"I'm a weed."

"You are *not*! Neither of us are weeds, Jo. We're the Highflyers, remember? Bill said so."

"Exactly. Highflyerssssss. Now I have to do a solo flight, and it's different."

"Not exactly solo. You'll have the Ancient Cobber along."

"Solo with unknown passenger," I said. "That makes it even worse."

"How long do you get to stay?" said Ruth. "Do you have to boomerang right back?"

"They're giving me a week. A week staying with one of *them*!"

"You can handle them. You'll probably wind up giving them a guided tour of Sydney."

"I know nothing about Australia. My ignorance is coast-to-coast comprehensive. I don't know a kangaroo from a wallaby – and I can't even spell kookaburra."

Judy Allen has written over 30 published titles. She has won the Earthworm Award, the Whitbread Children's novel Award and been Commended for the Carnegie Medal.

HIGHFLYERS

3

Sydney
Quest

Judy Allen

RED FOX

Quest Tours and Travel is a fictitious company and all the characters in this book are fictional.

A Red Fox Book

Published by Random House Children's Books
20 Vauxhall Bridge Road, London SW1V 2SA

A division of Random House UK Ltd
London Melbourne Sydney Auckland
Johannesburg and agencies throughout the world

1 3 5 7 9 10 8 6 4 2

First published simultaneously in
hardback and paperback by
Julia MacRae and Red Fox 1996

Phototypeset by Intype London Ltd
Printed and bound in Great Britain by
Cox & Wyman Ltd, Reading, Berkshire

RANDOM HOUSE UK Limited Reg. No. 954009

Papers used by Random House UK Limited
are natural, recyclable products made from wood
grown in sustainable forests. The manufacturing
processes conform to the environmental regulations
of the country of origin.

ISBN 0 09 955831 9

CONTENTS

1	Battle Plans	1
2	One Bear Short of a Picnic	9
3	A Grizzly Day at the Office	16
4	Orders from Abroad	23
5	Ruth Hatches a Plot	32
6	Appointment at Hallowe'en	40
7	. . . Your Flight is now Boarding . . .	49
8	A Desperate Man	54
9	The Reunion	63
10	A Date with Sydney Harbour	73
11	News of the Numbat	83
12	Mitch Missing	89
13	A Slight Misunderstanding	99
14	The End of the Line	107
15	Mitch's Secret	115

For Alice

CHAPTER ONE

Battle Plans

It was party-time in the Quest Travel offices – but dancing was not on the agenda. Signing up for holidays was on the agenda. So my father hoped.

Every year, as soon as the leaves begin to fall, my parents start to lay down battle plans for the following year.

My mother runs Quest Tours – Planned Package Holidays for People who are Seeking Something. My father runs Quest Travel – a travel agency which operates from the same building.

When Mum lays down battle plans she flies all over the world, working out unusual routes, checking eating places, river trips, hang-gliding facilities, haunted castles, discos, that kind of thing.

When Dad lays down battle plans he stays in the office organizing Promotional Events.

I'm spending my year out between school and college working for both of them, so, theoretically, I could be expeditioning with Mum. I'm a realist, though. I guessed right away which one of them I'd be helping.

By the time Ruth looked in I'd finished putting up the posters. Mick and Liz had cleared the desks and were sorting brochures. Peggy had the beers and wine stashed in the coolboxes and was starting to lay out the food. Bill was unpacking glasses.

Bill works for Mum, in Quest Tours upstairs, but when Dad's doing a promotion anyone who's passing has to help. Dad himself just stands in the middle of the front office, pointing and issuing orders. Until the customers arrive.

He looked a bit peeved when Ruth rapped on the street door. Especially as she had George with her. George is her half-brother and he's also about half her age which makes Dad wary of him. He pretends to think all the young are disruptive. Even though he knows George never is.

"If you've come to take Jo away, you can't, she's busy," he said. "But if you've come to help, you're welcome."

Ruth was quite startled. "I've never seen so many people working in here before," she said.

"That's because you've never been in at a busy time before," I said.

"It looks great!" said Ruth, taking in everything, turning her head this way and that way until her hair-beads rattled. "Come to Beautiful Canada, right? You want me to try for a Canadian accent to keep the theme going?"

"Your own'll do nicely," said Dad. "Very few people in Britain can tell the difference between East Coast American and Canadian anyway."

Bill picked up a tea-towel and flung it, with amazing accuracy, so it flopped over Ruth's shoulder. "No sightseers yet," he said. "Come and polish glasses or get thrown out."

Bill is the kind of man Ruth and I both think we

oughtn't to like, but neither of us can quite help it. He's thirty-something and he knows that he's good-looking and he knows he's charming and Ruth sometimes tells me she owes it to womankind to put him in his place. Trouble is, he's so good at being charming, she never quite gets around to it.

She pulled the tea-cloth off her shoulder and looked at it. "This throws the theme," she said. "It's got the Tower of London and Beefeaters on it."

"You won't be able to see the picture when you're using it," said Bill. He gave her one of his best lop-sided smiles. It never fails, not even on Ruth, and she picked up the nearest glass and began to dust it.

"I could do with some help carrying out the food," said Peggy plaintively, from the back kitchen behind the front office.

"There's food?" said George.

"Salmon and prawns," I said, "to go with the Canadian beer and wine."

"How can you tell if a salmon's Canadian?" said George, following me round the corner and squeezing into the kitchenette.

"It's not that hard, George," Ruth called after him. "You read the label on the freezer-pack."

"That's what I thought," said George. "But this one says 'Scotland' and it has a picture of a thistle on it."

"The wine and beer are genuine," said Peggy calmly. "We're not making any claims for the fish."

"That's cheating," said George sternly.

It's a good thing I like George. "There *are* salmon and prawns in Canada," I said, carrying out a dish and putting it on the counter. "It doesn't matter whether it's these specific ones or not."

"Well it can't be these ones, can it?" said George. "They're here."

I gave up and went back for the next dish.

"Niagara Falls!" said George dreamily, going to stand in front of one of our best posters. "I'd like to go over Niagara Falls in a barrel."

"You don't want to live to be eleven?" said Ruth.

"People have done it," said George. "I've read about it. You just have to keep your nerve."

"You also have to keep your body parts together while a million tons of water is pounding you against jagged rocks," said Ruth. "That's where most people come unstuck."

"Anyway," said George, still staring at the poster, "Canada looks brilliant. I'd really like to go."

"Why is it," said Ruth, "that advertising always works best on people who don't have any money."

She had just polished the last glass, dumped the tea-cloth into Bill's hands, and come over to lean on the counter by me, when the door opened – and Marina walked in.

Marina is an Italian tour operator. She is also totally stunning. That is the only possible word for it.

I knew she was in England, because I knew she was due to have a meeting with Dad the next morning, but I hadn't expected to see her before that.

The whole office went quiet for three seconds. Even George stared. Marina stood still for a moment, balancing perfectly on her high heels, and smiled at everyone in turn, ending with Bill. "I have this evening free," she announced. She speaks perfect English, with just enough of an accent to make anything she says sound interesting. "So I thought I would call in and say hallo."

"Your evening need not be free," said Bill, as soon as my father had finished the greetings and introductions. "We could have dinner together."

"That would be nice," said Marina.

"Boy, he works fast," Ruth whispered to me.

"They know each other," I whispered back. "Quest Tours has links with her company."

Bill has never actually tried his charm on me, but it's always been a bit of an education to see him swing into his act with other women. Now, though, it suddenly occurred to me that it would be a far better education to see how Marina works her magic on men.

I decided to watch and learn.

After three minutes I had worked out exactly how she does it. She does it by being beautiful, elegant, poised, expensively dressed – and smiling a lot.

Well – I can always try smiling a lot.

I gave up trying to learn from Marina and just got on with admiring her, like the rest of them.

Eventually, Bill arranged to collect her at her hotel later on and she swept gracefully out to the cab that was waiting at the kerb.

"Isn't she unreal?" said Bill, gazing after her.

"She looked pretty real to me!" said Ruth.

"She's an extremely efficient tour operator," said Dad briskly, as if he hadn't even noticed that she had other qualities as well.

"She has luminous eyes," said Bill dreamily.

"That's nice," said Ruth a bit louder. "In America we only have luminous bugs."

Bill just grinned and began to draw corks out of wine bottles.

I nudged Ruth and frowned at her. "Don't say

things like that," I said quietly. "It makes you sound jealous."

"I was trying to get you to lighten up," said Ruth. "I could see you going all invisible. Just like you did when Michelle showed up."

Sometimes, I find Ruth's efforts to boost my confidence very irritating.

"Michelle was a bit of a surprise," I said, "but I *didn't* try to be invisible! I behaved perfectly normally."

We'd been to Paris for a weekend, staying with Philippe. We had expected it to be the high-point of our year. Ruth has always said Philippe has a cuteness factor of around 100, and she was sure his friends would be just as interesting.

I suppose we should have guessed the glamorous Philippe would have a glamorous girl-friend, but for some reason we didn't. Michelle was really nice about having us along, but I have to say it wasn't quite the foursome we'd imagined.

"Admit it," I said to Ruth now. "You weren't expecting Michelle either."

"No, I wasn't," said Ruth, "but she was okay. I just thought they could have fixed us up with a couple of dates of our own."

"They didn't seem to think of it. Maybe the French aren't such a romantic nation after all."

"I guess they'd been cutting their Racial Stereotypes Night Classes," said Ruth. "Anyhow, the point I'm making is that you always look as though you feel inferior in the presence of beautiful women, and it drives me crazy. You are not inferior. Neither of us are."

"You saw Marina," I said. "And you can see me! Of course I feel inferior! What do you expect?"

"Pay attention!" said Ruth. "I would like you to reinterpret this experience in a more positive way."

"How?"

"If you *really* want to look like that," said Ruth, trying to sound as if no one in her right mind *would* want to, "then take notes about her clothes and cosmetics and *do* it. Otherwise, just be yourself. Remember – it's what's inside that counts."

"Yeah, Jo," said George, "so what did you have for lunch?"

"I mean inside her head and her heart, you doodle-brain," said Ruth, "not inside her stomach!"

"Thanks," I said, "but I don't remember writing in to the agony pages. If you must talk to me, talk about lumberjacks and mounties. I have to swing into the hard sell on the frozen north in about ten minutes."

"Why would people want to go to Canada now?" said Ruth. "It's cold there and it's cold here. Why aren't they heading for the sun?"

"That's for later," I said, happy to have got her off the subject of my self-confidence. "We tell them about the sun when they're depressed after Christmas. Now they're all thinking about skiing."

"Don't they go to the Alps for that?"

"They can," I said, "but Canada has *guaranteed* snow. They're willing to pay more and fly further for *guaranteed* snow."

"They are?"

"They may not be yet, but by the time this promotion's over they will be. Well, some of them will be – the rest are just here for the beer."

That made me think of something. "What are *you* here for?" I said. "I shouldn't really be talking to you – I'm supposed to be working."

"Yes, sorry," said Ruth, as casually as if she wasn't about to drop a bombshell. "I didn't know. I came by because I thought you'd have finished for the day. I wanted to ask if you'd like to come to New York with me."

CHAPTER TWO

One Bear Short of a Picnic

"What!"

"I *said*, I wondered if you'd like to come to New York with me?" said Ruth.

Every year since her parents broke up Ruth has spent some time in New York with her American father. This was the first time she'd planned to go for Christmas and the first time she'd suggested I might go too. My mind went into overdrive.

"I couldn't afford the fare," I said, "and anyway my parents might not like me being away at Christmas . . . I know you're going, but your mother still has George and George's father . . ."

"Hey, close the floodgates a minute," said Ruth. "I'm not going for the Christmas holidays after all. I'm going in a couple of weeks and staying on for Thanksgiving."

"What's changed?"

"My father's met someone new. It sounds serious. He's going to her folks for the Christmas holidays so he wants me to go out earlier."

"How do you feel about that?"

"It's cool. The only problem is that everyone I know over there will be working a lot of the time."

An inspiration struck me.

"You could get in touch with Edward," I said. "He'd love to hear from you – he was definitely interested – and he did give you his phone number."

Ruth shook her head and shrugged.

"He may not have been a superstar," I said, "but you *must* remember Ed the Vet!"

"I do remember him," said Ruth. "I also remember his family. I think I may give him a miss."

We'd met Edward in Amsterdam, where we were acting as temporary couriers. It was true that his father was a rich, lecherous New York banker, his mother was a basilisk and his sister was a walking cosmetics ad – but Ed had seemed nice. Quiet and nice.

"Anyhow, Ed's in veterinary school," said Ruth. "He'll be busy, too. I don't mind hanging out on my own – it's just that it would be much better if you could be there. We could have a great time, Jo."

"I don't know how much I can push it," I said. "I've already had two trips to Paris and one to Amsterdam."

"Amsterdam was work," said Ruth reasonably enough, "and so was the first Paris trip, kind of – and the second one didn't count. This is meant to be our year out from real life, Jo, this is the year we rave around the world together."

"I know, and I don't think I've quite got it right," I said. "I have to earn the money before I can rave, and I don't have time to rave while I'm earning."

"Hey, Ruth, you could take me," said George. "I'm terrific company."

"School," said Ruth. "You know you can't take time out."

"You never take me at Christmas, either," said George.

"Oh George," said Ruth, putting her arm round him, "I'm sorry, but it's not as if you never get to America – Mom's taken you twice now."

"But we go to California!" said George.

"Oh, hey, you poor kid," said Ruth, removing her arm from his shoulders and giving him a shove. "Having grandparents in California! Being forced to visit the ocean and the surfing beaches and the redwoods, what a horrible life you do have."

"It's not New York," said George stubbornly. "It's not the same. If Jo can take time out of work I can take time out of school."

"But Jo can't," I said. "I'm not going either, George, so don't feel left out."

"Don't give up so easily," said Ruth.

"I'll ask," I said, "but I know what the answer'll be. It's all right for you, you haven't got a job anyway."

"Thanks for reminding me," said Ruth quietly.

"I'm sorry," I said. I felt awful. I knew how hard Ruth had tried to get work. "I know it isn't your fault."

"It's okay," said Ruth, "this change of vacation date works really well for me. It means I'll be here through December and I'm bound to be able to get casual work in a store around that time."

"I'll miss you while you're away!" I said.

"Never mind," said Ruth. "Tom is due over here soon, isn't he? That's something to look forward to!"

George lost interest and wandered off. I pretended to lose interest and shrugged. "Oh, I've forgotten all about him," I said casually.

"Jo! He was a dream on legs! You can't have!"

11

I hadn't, of course, but I'd been hoping Ruth had. There are some things you don't want to admit, even to your best friend. Especially if she has a steady boyfriend, *and* could have fifty more if she wanted, and you don't.

You don't want to admit you're interested in someone in case it doesn't work out. It's that simple.

When we met Tom in Paris and he seemed to like me and said he'd take me out when he visited London, I played it cool. For one thing he's Australian and it's not easy to have a relationship with someone who lives on the other side of the world. For another thing, I was sure he'd forget me the second I was out of his sight.

I played it cool with Tom, I played it cool with Ruth, I even played it cool with myself. And I was still playing it cool. I hadn't even told Ruth that I'd found out something that made my date with Tom about as likely as Christmas in June. I just didn't want to talk about it.

Fortunately, something happened that distracted everyone. There was a thud on the street door. Mick opened it and a motorcycle courier tottered in carrying a huge cardboard box.

George scuffed outside to take a look at the bike.

"Right, folks," said Dad, beginning to tear at the packaging on the box. "Action stations in a few minutes."

"I'm off," said Bill, blowing a kiss at the office in general.

"But you're not meeting Marina for another hour and a half," I said, surprised.

"I'll pick her up early," said Bill. "I want to get well clear in case the suit fits."

He strode out, almost colliding with George who was coming back in.

"What *was* he talking about?" said Ruth.

"I've been trying not to think about it," I said, as Dad began to haul something out of the packaging. "My father has gone temporarily out of his mind."

"What's he done?" said Ruth. "What *is* that? It looks like something died in that box."

"He's ordered a grizzly bear outfit and someone is going to have to put it on and walk round carrying a tray of drinks," I said through clenched teeth. "We at Quest Travel are full of enterprise. We'll stop at nothing to promote the land of mountains, lakes and forests."

"You're right, he *is* crazy," said Ruth. "His logic's gone. The point about Canadian bears is that you *don't* share your picnic with them – or only by accident, anyway."

"You misunderstand," said my father, standing upright and shaking out something large and fluffy. "This is about photo opportunities. We'll only get a decent-sized piece in the local paper if there's a picture and no one wants a shot of me standing under a poster of the Rocky Mountains. But *this* . . ."

He held up the suit triumphantly. Then his face fell.

Out of all the people in the office, my father was the only one who didn't laugh. "Get that courier back," he said. "Where is he? Is the bike still outside?"

"He's gone," said George. "He'll be miles away by now."

They had sent the wrong bear.

We had been expecting something dark brown and

13

serious-looking, with a muzzle and claws. They had sent something golden and snub-nosed, with soft paws and a bow round its neck. We had put in an order for a Grizzly. We had taken delivery of a Teddy.

"I'll get on to the shop," said Peggy, picking up the phone. "They definitely have the right suit – I checked and double checked. Someone just packed the wrong one, that's all."

"Jo, get a cab," said my father. "Get over there at once, give them back this – this *thing* – and get the right one. The photographer is due in about half an hour."

"Come for the ride," I said to Ruth, "for old time's sake. Our third good deed for Quest!"

"Sure," said Ruth. While I grabbed my bag she took the large, golden, furry suit out of my father's hands. "It's not quite up to our usual standard, though, is it? Doing a mercy dash through the streets of London with an empty soft toy?"

"It'll save the day," I said, pushing her ahead of me onto the street where Mick was already flagging down a cab for us. "And that definitely *is* our style."

Ruth struggled into the back of the cab and settled the sagging bear on her lap so its head flopped onto her shoulder. "Don't feel bad about this," she said to it, stroking its ears. "It isn't your fault. I'm sure you'll get to go to a party soon."

I climbed in after her, Dad shoved the packaging into my arms and slammed the door, and the cab roared off.

"I don't mind being used as a messenger," I said, "but I can tell you one thing I'm *not* doing, whatever anyone says."

"What's that?" said Ruth.

"I'm *not* wearing the thing," I said. "I don't care what size it is, I don't care if it fits me better than anyone else in the universe, I am positively, definitely and finally *not* wearing it."

CHAPTER THREE

A Grizzly Day at the Office

"Is it very stuffy in there?" said Ruth sympathetically.

"It's horrible," I said. "It smells. And I can't breathe. It's like having a pillow over your face."

"It's hard to hear what you say," said Ruth. "You sound as if you have a pillow over your face."

I will never believe I was the only one that bear outfit would fit. They all ganged up on me. Dad and Mick claimed to be too tall. Liz said she was too wide. Peggy demanded exemption on the grounds of her great age, which was rubbish because she's not that much older than Mum. Mum, of course, was somewhere in Spain. Bill had fled.

Even Ruth, who is exactly the same size as me, suddenly 'remembered' she had an allergy to fur, all fur, even tatty synthetic fur. The only person who really wanted to be zipped into the battered old grizzly suit was George, and he was too short.

The bear had glassy brown eyes but they were not designed so I could look out through them. I was expected to see through the mouth, which was slightly open. It gave a very narrow view. Also the teeth got in the way. I had to breathe and speak

16

through a bit of gauzy stuff let into the throat and camouflaged with fur.

They had wisely decided not to trust me to walk round with the drinks after all. Instead, I stood in a corner of Quest Travel, with a set of Canadian skiing brochures clutched against my hairy chest, swinging my head around to try and get a general view of the room.

"Could you cut down the head movements a bit?" came Dad's voice. "You look as though you're hallucinating."

I scanned around to find him. Then I tipped my head back and leant forwards so I could get his face in focus between my two rows of fangs.

"Don't *do* that!" said Dad. "The clients'll think you're going to bite. You're supposed to be endearing not rabid."

"We *had* endearing," said Ruth sternly. "You made us take endearing back to the shop. This is mean. This is the bear that finds you in the parking lot and wrecks your car if you don't give it all the cookies."

"Well, just try and stand reasonably still for the press photographer," said Dad.

I nodded vigorously. The ski brochures set off on a kind of slalom course down my furry arms, across my paws, and off the end of the foot I stuck out instinctively to try and control them.

"I just hope Tom doesn't pick this evening to show," said Ruth, gathering them up. "He specifically told you he doesn't like women to dress up for him."

"Very funny," I growled, allowing her to arrange my arms like a sort of tray and balance the brochures on them. "Fortunately he wouldn't recognise me."

"He might if he looked in your mouth and saw

17

your eyes," said Ruth. "You have quite distinctive eyes."

"And I probably wouldn't recognise him, either," I said, trying to play the whole thing down.

"Sure you would," said Ruth. "Tall, blond, athletic . . ."

"You have a fixation with him," I said. "He's in the past."

I had thought right from the beginning that the whole Tom thing was too good to be true. When I discovered, two days before I was turned into a bear, that it *had* been too good to be true, I decided not to mention it to Ruth. I knew she'd be kind and sympathetic about it – and I thought I might very likely burst into tears.

I must have been mad to think Ruth would let the subject drop. She had been so pleased that my luck seemed to have changed.

I had pointed out to her that the best I could hope for – the *very* best – was two days of happiness and then heartbreak. How can you keep a relationship going if one of you lives in London and the other in Sydney?

Ruth had said that didn't matter. Her theory seemed to be that a romance with someone like Tom, however brief and doomed, would give me so much confidence that I would instantly attract someone else.

"You have the dates for his London visit, don't you?" she persisted. "It *is* around now, isn't it?"

I realised I'd have to fill her in or she'd never stop.

"You remember Tom's aunts?" I said.

"How could I forget the Power Women?" said Ruth.

"Well they've booked themselves some extra city days," I said, "in Europe. They're travelling home direct from Frankfurt. They've cut out their London visit. No time. And Tom is travelling with them. So – romance over before it began, okay?"

"But I thought there was some reason they *had* to come back," said Ruth. "Some ancient relation over here they had to meet up with for the flight back to Oz?"

"Well, they're not coming," I said. "I've seen the bookings, Ruth. London doesn't feature at all, for any of them."

"That's terrible," said Ruth. "I can't believe it. Jo, I am so sorry!"

"And the really ironic bit," I said, "is that the only reason they decided to extend their European tour is because I gave them such a good time in Paris. You always said I shouldn't use my initiative. Well, you were right. Excuse me, I'm tired of being a stationary bear, I'm going to be a dancing bear."

Whatever Ruth or anyone else might say on the subject, I was determined to stay calm and aloof. I just needed a bit of time to get in the mood.

I lurched off across the room, balancing my brochures surprisingly well, and managing some quite interesting steps considering the short, hairy legs I was stuck with.

The clients laughed and ducked out of my way and spilt their prawns. The photographer's bulb flashed. Dad gave a jaunty little interview promising he'd have good deals on Canadian holidays available for at least a couple more weeks. And people began to make bookings.

By the time I'd finished my dance, and was sagging

against a wall being stroked by a baby in someone's backpack, I was almost fainting with heat. But I could tell by the general noise, and the tone of Dad's voice, that the evening was a success.

"You were brilliant!" said George's voice. I couldn't get him in my sights but I was aware he was patting me on the arm.

"Terrific!" said Ruth, from the other side of me. "Your father is obviously going to achieve his ambition of transporting the whole of London across the Atlantic."

"I may not be lucky in love," I said, "but when it comes to the travel business I do have my moments."

"It's okay," said Ruth. "I've taken the hint. I won't mention Tom again."

Never let anyone tell you there's no such thing as a coincidence. There has to be or there wouldn't be a word for it. Right at that moment we had a really big one.

From somewhere in the general confusion, in a voice that carried above all the other voices and managed to get right through the fur over my ears, Peggy called my name. "Jo," she called, "Jo – over here. It's Tom."

Did I stay calm and aloof as planned? Not exactly. I shrieked, threw the brochures on the floor and ripped my head off.

Two seconds later I regretted it. I had been anonymous, now I was recognisable. What was worse, I could tell that my face was red and sweaty and my hair was damp and crushed.

"Relax!" said Peggy, as I lumbered over to her, looking wildly in all directions. "He's not here in

20

person, he's on the telephone." She held the receiver
out to me.

I took it and waited for a moment until my breathing was more or less back to normal. Then I put it
to my ear and said, "Hi." I didn't want to overdo the
greeting.

"Hi," said Tom's voice. "How're you doing? Sorry
about the background noise – I'm at Geneva
Airport."

"Oh," I said. Then, deciding there was really no
point in being cool any more, "I'm really sorry you're
not coming to London after all."

"Oh well," said Tom and he laughed. "You lose
some, you win some. The aunts said I should call
you to tell you it's okay by me."

"What is?"

"Has the fax arrived?"

"Not that I know of. What fax?"

"It'll be there," said Tom. "I just wanted to say,
no worries. It's a neat idea. So don't be embarrassed
or anything, okay? Hey, I have to go, they're calling
the Milan flight. See ya."

The line went dead.

"See you," I said weakly and too late.

"Is he in London?" said Ruth, coming round
behind the counter and watching as I hung up.

"No, he's in the departure lounge of a Swiss
Airport."

"So what did he say?"

"I don't know."

"Sorry," said Ruth, "I'll back off. It was private,
right?"

"No," I said. "I mean, I *really* don't know. He said
everything was okay and I mustn't be embarrassed.

21

And something about a fax. I think he got a wrong number. I think he thought he was speaking to some other girl."

"A fax is coming through now," said Peggy.

It was addressed to my father. Normally Peggy would have let me see it. No one sends a personal message by fax to an office.

But my father was passing the machine as it slid through. He tore off the sheet, stared at it, and said, "I haven't time to deal with this now." Then he shoved it into his pocket and got on with booking a group of four onto a Toronto flight.

"What was it?" I said to Peggy.

"Did you catch any of it?" said Ruth.

"Not much," said Peggy. "But your name was mentioned more than once, Jo. Try to get your father's attention as soon as you can. Whatever it is, I'm certain it has something to do with you."

She was right. It certainly did have something to do with me.

CHAPTER FOUR

Orders from Abroad

There is a reason why I didn't find out what was in the fax until the next day.

The promotion went well, which meant it also went on late. I was still in costume long after Ruth had taken George away. When the last clients finally staggered out of the door, Peggy offered to run me home and Dad told me to go. He said he wanted to finish the clearing up before he left.

I was so shattered I went straight to bed as soon as Peggy had driven off. I planned to stay awake until Dad got in, but I crashed so totally I didn't even hear him leave the next morning. The first thing I was aware of was the telephone ringing at about eight.

"So what's the story?" came Ruth's voice as soon as I lifted the receiver.

She was not impressed to hear that I didn't know.

"How could anyone be so wiped?" she said. "It didn't go on *that* late!"

"I've had a heavy week," I said, feeling distinctly irritated. "We've been supplying the latest Quest Tours and Travel leaflets to hotels. We hook Australians and Americans who've flown direct to Britain and decided to sort out the rest of Europe from here.

That's how the Power Women got on to Quest in the first place."

"Well ask your father now!" said Ruth. "I'm curious even if you're not."

"He's gone already. He promised me a lie-in today."

"It *would* be today!" said Ruth.

"The sooner you let me off the phone," I said, "the sooner I can dress and get down there."

"Fair enough," said Ruth. "Let's meet for lunch. But remember I am a really cheap person. I hate to spend money. Especially as I haven't got any."

"The pizza place?"

"You got it!" said Ruth. "We can share a deep-pan, with nothing on the side, and drink tap-water. I can run to that. But you *will* have found out what gives, won't you? I'm not good at being patient."

I said I'd noticed that.

To be truthful, I wasn't as laid back myself as I was pretending to be. I was down at the Agency before nine. Much to my father's surprise. He'd expected me to take half the morning off because of last night.

By the time I reached the restaurant I knew exactly what the fax had been about.

"It was from Mrs Cooper," I said.

"The Senior Power Woman," said Ruth, saluting.

"She doesn't want her aged relative to fly out to Oz on his own," I said. "She wants him to have an escort." I left a suitably dramatic pause. "And she wants it to be me."

Ruth slammed the palms of her hands on the table, making half the restaurant jump. "Brilliant!" she said. "Great! Excellent! I *knew* it was something like that."

The waitress dumped the pizza between us. "I brought it as fast as I could," she said sourly.

"It's okay," said Ruth. "That was joy, not hostility."

"So is everything all right?" said the waitress suspiciously. Her voice was no friendlier.

"Everything is perfect, thank you," said Ruth. "Everything is magic."

The waitress retreated, looking both cross and mystified.

"I'm so happy for you," said Ruth. "You may not be going to make it to New York, but at least you get to travel – and how!"

"They're mad, of course," I said.

"Why?"

"They don't need to pay for someone like me to sit beside him. They could have put him in the care of the airline. He'd have been fine."

"Guilt," said Ruth, dividing the pizza carefully. "They can't go with him themselves because they're too busy being self-indulgent. And when the rich feel guilty they spend more money. It's a well-documented psychological fact."

She began to eat her pizza slice in her fingers. I took a knife and fork to mine. We may be best friends, but that doesn't mean there aren't cultural differences.

"There's just one thing," said Ruth, nipping off a long, gluey string of cheese with her front teeth, "that I don't understand about this. I'm the one who's *not* going. So how come I'm the one who's excited?"

"I'm just being businesslike," I said. "I am excited really." And I was. In fact I was quite dazed with excitement.

I also had another emotion going on, but I couldn't quite pin it down at that stage.

"It'll be a bit scary, though, won't it?" said Ruth. "Being in charge of a crumbly?"

"Not really," I said. "The in-flight staff'll take charge if he starts to disintegrate."

"It's a *long* way away," said Ruth.

"I know. I *have* seen an atlas!"

"It's on the other side of the planet!" said Ruth.

That was when I realised what the other emotion was. Fear.

"You're making me nervous," I said.

"Sorry," said Ruth, and her eyes went unfocused as she tried to think of something reassuring to say. "It *is* only a small planet. It's not like you live on Jupiter and have to get to the other side of *that*."

"It will be a little weird," I said, "now I think about it. I'll look up at the sky and I won't even see the same stars."

"So don't look up."

"And the bath water'll go down the plughole the wrong way."

"Take showers and don't look down."

"You've flushed out the truth," I said. "I'm a weed."

"You are *not*!"

"I am. I'm all talk. I should have walked out of the school gates, put my stuff in a backpack, and worked my way round the world – instead of hanging around the family travel business hoping to be sent somewhere interesting."

"Working your way round the world isn't as easy as it sounds," said Ruth. "Especially as half of it's a war zone."

"It doesn't even *sound* easy to me."

"Fear is like an ocean wave," said Ruth. "You have to ride it like a surfer, not let it overwhelm you. I read that on a desk calendar once."

"I still say I'm a weed."

"Neither of us are weeds, Jo. We're the Highflyers, remember? Bill said so."

"Exactly. Highflyersssssss. Now I have to do a solo flight, and it's different."

"Not exactly solo. You'll have the Ancient Cobber along."

"Solo with unknown passenger," I said. "That makes it even worse."

"How long do you get to stay?" said Ruth. "Do you have to boomerang right back?"

"They're giving me a week. A week staying with one of *them*!"

"You can handle them. You'll probably wind up giving them a guided tour of Sydney."

"I know nothing about Australia. My ignorance is coast-to-coast comprehensive. I don't know a kangaroo from a wallaby – and I can't even spell kookaburra."

"You only have to visit," said Ruth. "You're not expected to label the wildlife. On to important things! You'll get a whole week with Tom." She frowned. "This must be what he was talking about when he rang – but why did he say you mustn't be embarrassed? Why would you be?"

"I suppose he was letting me know he understood the plan," I said. "Letting me know he wouldn't think I was chasing him or anything."

Ruth clinked her glass of water against mine. "Let's

pretend this is champagne," she said. "Here's to a fantastic seven days."

The second of Mrs Cooper's faxes was waiting when Ruth and I got back to the Agency in search of a free coffee.

It was to tell me, via my father of course, that perhaps I ought to know that Mr Mitchell was eighty and, therefore, somewhat confused. The next door neighbour was dealing with everything, but I ought to meet her, and also meet Mr Mitchell himself, well in advance of the trip. And I must understand that my responsibility began the moment he left his own front door and did not end until he was in her car at Sydney Airport.

"It gets worse," I said.

Ruth kept her cheerful smile going as she read over my shoulder. "You knew you'd have to pay for your fun," she said. "But once you get him there – you can let the good times roll."

We were still staring at the piece of paper when the fax machine went into action.

"For me again?" I said.

"No," said Peggy, reading it as it came through. "It's for your father again – but it *is* from Mrs Cooper and it *is* about you."

"Read it," my father called through from the back room. "It's your assignment now. You deal with it."

"It's infuriating," I said. "Why doesn't she start addressing stuff to me?"

"Because she's the kind of woman who only ever deals with the person at the top," said Ruth.

"She was happy enough to deal with us in Paris," I said. "They both were. In fact they insisted on it."

"In Paris we were all they had," said Ruth. "A

traveller dying of thirst will drink from a stagnant puddle."

"If that comes from the same calendar, I think you should get rid of it. It's having a bad effect on your brain."

The third fax was to say that Mrs Cooper had decided I might need to know something about her uncle. "He is probably far more nervous about coming home than he will admit to you," she wrote. "He fell out with his father when he was young, and left Australia. He hasn't been back since. That's more than fifty years. The feud with his father was never resolved, not even when the old man died. I pass on these personal details because it seems only fair to give you a chance of understanding some of his ramblings."

"Not only do I have to be a babysitter," I said uneasily, "I have to babysit someone with a past."

"He's eighty, Jo," said Ruth. "He couldn't *not* have a past."

Mick came out of the kitchenette with a tray of coffee.

"Is Bill upstairs?" said Ruth, sounding ultra-casual. "I'll take one up to him."

"No need," I said. "We just shout and he comes down for it."

Surprisingly, Ruth took no notice. She just took a mug off the tray and went upstairs, carrying it carefully so it wouldn't spill.

I hardly had time to notice that this was a bit out of character when the office suddenly got incredibly busy. I'm not qualified to do bookings, but I can start people off and hand them over to someone else when it begins to get serious.

There was no time to think while the rush went on. It was only when it was over that I realised what a long time Ruth had been gone. And, because the rush *was* over and it was quiet, I couldn't help hearing what she said as she came out of Bill's office a few moments later. What she said was, "With your charm, you can do anything." Then they both laughed.

When she ran downstairs again I felt I wanted to say something. But what? How could I say to my best friend 'He's too old for you, he isn't suitable' without sounding as if I thought I was her mother? How could I say I was sure that falling for Bill would be like falling for a vampire – sooner or later he'd flap off after someone else, leaving her all pale and washed up.

I tried to tell myself I was over-reacting. She'd only had a coffee with him, after all. But I couldn't help worrying.

Mrs Cooper's fourth fax came through just after Bill himself had clattered downstairs and made enthusiastic noises about what he called 'the Aussie business'.

Naturally, I didn't admit to him what I had admitted to Ruth over our pizza, about fear being among my reactions. I just grinned and tore off the fax.

As I turned back from the machine I caught a look that passed between the two of them. It was a kind of grin and wink. It looked almost as if they were nudging each other, though they were at opposite ends of the counter. I could tell I wasn't meant to see – so I pretended I hadn't.

It was silly, but on top of feeling anxious for her I also felt betrayed. Ruth and I always told each other everything. We'd certainly agreed what we both thought about Bill. Now it seemed she'd changed her mind about him, in a very unsettling way, without saying anything to me at all.

I read the fax aloud.

It said: 'There is something I keep forgetting to mention to Jo. My uncle is all kinds of chauvinist. Among the things he is prejudiced against are the young, the English and females. There is no way he would agree to be escorted to Sydney by a young English female. So I have told him that *he* is escorting *her*. I thought it would make things simpler for Jo if I provided her with a reason for her trip. So I have told my uncle that she is Tom's girl-friend, eager to visit him but nervous of the journey. I rely on her to keep up the subterfuge.'

I clutched Ruth's arm. "*Now* I know why Tom told me not to be embarrassed," I said. "But he might as well not have bothered. I am very embarrassed indeed. This is *awful*!"

CHAPTER FIVE

Ruth Hatches a Plot

Once the first shock wore off, I managed to calm myself down. Pretending to be Tom's girl-friend was a job, I told myself, that was all. And Tom himself had said, "No worries."

Anyhow, there were practical things to think about. Getting a visa and looking through my clothes, for example.

It would be very uncool to arrive with more than one piece of luggage. I didn't want to behave like a tourist and pack everything I owned 'just in case'. I wanted to be selective – but it was hard to decide what to select.

I knew it would be spring in Australia, but the main problem wasn't the climate, it was that I didn't know what kind of week I was going to have. I had no idea what I'd be doing.

Looking back, it's probably a good thing I didn't know, but at that stage it was annoying.

Ruth tried to help. "Take something to swim in and something to party in," she said.

"We may not do anything like that," I said. "This is an invented relationship, don't forget. Tom may ignore me. I could spend the whole time sightseeing alone."

"So pack what you wear for city tours," said Ruth.

"The guidebook says not to wear perfume or cosmetics. That should lighten the load."

"Why would it say that?"

"Apparently they attract insects."

"What are you telling me!" said Ruth. "We've watched the soaps, we know Australian women wear make-up. Are you saying they're all covered with flies or what?"

"Well of course not! They wouldn't have flies in the studio!"

"Not if they didn't have passes, I guess," said Ruth. "Look, it's easy. You just need four kinds of gear. The first for if it's cooler than you think – the second for if it's hotter than you hoped – the third to have a good time in and the fourth to be stood up in."

I ignored her and continued to pack and unpack, make lists and tear them up again.

I also contacted Mr Mitchell's next door neighbour, Mrs Frost. She suggested I should go down for afternoon tea. It was only after we'd agreed the day and time that I realised it would be Hallowe'en. I'm not quite sure why, but that seemed somehow appropriate.

My father said I could take the car. I was really pleased – and quite surprised. We only have one car between the three of us so I hardly ever get to use it. This would be the longest run I'd ever made.

"You've earned it," said Dad. "You're doing a very good PR job for Quest. I can't help thinking most of it's been luck and accident, but I'm still willing to give you some credit."

Ruth volunteered to come for the ride. She doesn't drive – her family doesn't have a car for environmental reasons – but I thought it would be nice to have company. Especially at what Ruth called The Mad Cobber's Tea Party.

It wasn't until I got into the office on the 31st that I realised there was something really important I should do. I should ask for some details about Tom.

I checked the schedule to see where Mrs Cooper and her party had got to. They were still in Milan. I looked up the fax number of the hotel and wrote a short note. It felt really strange, doing that, especially as I thought he might read it. But I didn't see how I could pretend to be his girl-friend when I didn't even know the most basic things about him.

By the time Ruth turned up I still hadn't had an answer from Italy.

I couldn't decide whether to send another fax or not. To take my mind off the decision I was cutting the ties on some packs of new brochures and sorting them ready to send to some of our regulars.

Ruth said, "That's cool. I'm early. Carry on." So I did.

When I'd finished and looked round, there was no sign of her.

"She went upstairs," said Peggy.

There was nobody upstairs but Bill.

I stamped up to his office with a heavy feeling in my chest. It seemed I hadn't been imagining things. It seemed Ruth really was hooked by Bill's high-octane charisma.

In one way I couldn't believe it. In another way I couldn't see how *not* to believe it.

I would like to mention at this point that I didn't

stamp because I was angry. I stamped so they'd hear me. I would have hated to walk in quietly and see them spring apart.

Ruth was on her way to the door to meet me as I reached it. So I couldn't tell how close they'd been before. But I thought her eyes were suspiciously bright and Bill was looking extremely pleased with himself. He usually does, but this was more so.

"How come someone who doesn't wear Doc Martens can make such a noise on the stairs?" said Ruth.

"Sorry," I said, "just trying to get your attention. I think we should go."

The fax came through just as Ruth and I reached the ground floor. It was from Mrs Cooper, and for a wonder it was actually addressed to me.

It was very short – totally useless – and slightly offensive. It said: "You have all the information you need. Just remember that Mr Mitchell is escorting you, not the other way about. The story about you being Tom's girl-friend is simply an alibi in case of need. My uncle will not remember any of that, nor will he be interested. I very much doubt if it will need to be referred to again."

It ended with something which didn't make any sense to me, but as I had read the rest aloud to Ruth, I read that bit as well. "We accept the terms," I read, "including the RTW ticket."

The sentence had the most extraordinary effect on Ruth. Her face went bright pink, clashing slightly with her red hair.

Then she yelled for Bill to come downstairs.

Before his foot was off the bottom step she was nudging me and telling me to read the fax aloud again.

I did. And even though I know what RTW stands for, I still didn't understand what was going on.

To my total astonishment, Ruth and Bill flung themselves into each other's arms and hugged. Publicly.

"What?" I said.

Then Ruth hugged me. Half a second later Bill hugged me. Before I had time to notice, crossly, that this seemed to have the effect of liquidising my kneecaps, Peggy hurried over and hugged me, too.

"It was a corporate effort," said Ruth. "I had the idea! Bill fixed it with the Power Women! Peggy talked your father into agreeing as long as they did! And it worked! They're not buying you a return to Sydney! They're buying you a Round-The-World ticket. You fly back the other way and stop over at JFK!"

"What!" I said, too amazed to come up with anything original.

"We've cracked it!" said Ruth. "We get a whole week together in New York!"

My father mooched out of the back office. "I think I deserve a hug, too," he said mildly. "I'm giving you two weeks out of the office – only one of which is legitimate work!"

I obliged.

Then he tapped his watch face sternly and said, "They'll be putting the kettle on in Surrey soon. You should get moving."

For the first half of the drive Ruth and I were talking so much about New York that I quite forgot Mrs Cooper's somewhat stinging remark about me and Tom. Then I remembered it.

"She certainly doesn't want me to take advantage of her nephew, does she," I said.

"Doesn't matter what she wants," said Ruth calmly. "It's what you and Tom want. At least it looks as though you're not going to have to keep up a charade with old Uncle Oz."

"What *am* I going to say to him, though?"

"Talk about the weather," said Ruth. "Like the English always do. Not that it matters – you've been told he's totally confused."

I should have known better, but I allowed myself to be comforted by that.

It was a beautiful drive. The leaves on the trees were all shades of red and yellow and we kept passing infant witches and baby ghosts being led off to Hallowe'en parties.

"It's the tea-time ghouls," said Ruth. "The tall, scary ones don't come out till later. Look at that dinosaur! Is that cute, or is that cute?"

"I can't look," I said sternly, "I'm steering a small metal room on wheels. And speaking of cute – I have a confession to make. I thought you'd fallen under Bill's spell."

"Oh please!" said Ruth. "Don't you know me better than that?"

"He does have something about him," I said, remembering the hug.

"I know," said Ruth and giggled. "He hugged me, too, remember!"

"How did you know what I was thinking?"

"I usually do," said Ruth. "But I'm not about to join a queue behind Marina. I guess he has half a dozen girl-friends already, hasn't he?"

"Half a dozen and one I think. But most of them

are tour operators or couriers or air hostesses so there's not much chance they'll meet each other."

"That's what I'd have expected," said Ruth. "He's a class-act, but you should know I'm not dumb enough to take all that flirty stuff seriously."

"The others do. And they're older than you – and very sophisticated."

"You can't get around me like that. You know I'd tell you if Bill was on my hit list. I was hatching a plot, that's all. For *your* benefit."

"You could have got Peggy to sort the whole thing," I said.

I realised a very faint flicker of suspicion was still lurking in my head.

"Peggy is great," said Ruth, "but think about it. Who in Quest is the ideal person to charm an expensive ticket out of two middle-aged women?"

"You're right, of course," I said. The flicker of suspicion went out.

"I'm always right," said Ruth. "Now let me concentrate on this map if you want me to navigate you to the castle of the Aussie Ogre."

"This is going to be a tricky meeting," I said as I parked, almost straight, in front of Mr Mitchell's house. "I'm nervous, but I need to act confident to keep myself going. I can do that all right, but I have to remember Mr Mitchell thinks I'm too scared to fly alone, so now I have to work out how to act nervous without making myself *really* nervous. So what we have here is a nervous person acting like a confident person who's acting like a nervous person. Does that make sense?"

"No," said Ruth.

Mrs Frost opened the door to Mr Mitchell's house.

"It's so nice of you to come down," she said. "He's looking forward to meeting you. I expect you know the house is as good as sold and the stuff he's taking to Sydney is already on its way by sea. Also I've made sure his travel papers are in order. I don't think you'll be able to check them – that would rather give things away. He's quite sure *he's* taking *you*."

"He does remember that, does he?" I said.

"Yes," said Mrs Frost, looking faintly surprised.

"We were told he was a little – confused," said Ruth.

"Who told you that?" said Mrs Frost.

"Mrs Cooper," I said.

"Oh?" said Mrs Frost. "Well, I can't say I've noticed it. Anyway, come on in and meet him."

She guided us across the hall, opened a door and ushered us into a room.

A tall, white-haired man, who was definitely old but not nearly as decrepit as we'd expected, was getting rather stiffly to his feet from an armchair.

He stared at us without smiling. Then he began to walk slowly towards us, leaning on a stick, looking from one to the other with very bright blue eyes.

"So which of you is Tom's new girl?" he said. "Let's have a look at you – see if he's got good taste or not."

CHAPTER SIX

Appointment at Hallowe'en

The Hallowe'en tea party was even more unnerving than going into an exam unprepared. At least if it's an exam you know what's the worst thing that can happen. You can fail.

But I had no idea what would happen if I blew it that afternoon in Mr Mitchell's house in deepest Surrey.

Would he refuse to travel with me? Would he refuse to travel at all? Would the Power Women blacken the name of Quest throughout the Southern Hemisphere?

I knew I was in trouble when he started off by asking which of us was Tom's girl-friend. This was not the ancient, forgetful old boy I'd been promised. This was a man who definitely knew what day of the week it was, and wanted to make sure I did, too.

"I assume Tom picked the red-head?" he said. He was looking us over as if we were in a pet shop – and probably not worth buying.

My spirits dropped a little.

Then my red-headed companion jerked her thumb in my direction and said tersely, "Jo is Tom's friend. My name's Ruth."

I could tell by her tone that she had not taken to my client.

My spirits dropped a little more. A trouble shared can be a trouble doubled – and don't let anyone tell you different.

Ruth was even less pleased when Mr Mitchell peered at me and said, "It seems you're not capable of going anywhere alone! Even in England!"

I grabbed her arm, hoping to shut her up. Then I smiled and said, "It's very kind of you to let me travel to Sydney with you."

"Go and sit down," said Mr Mitchell. "I want to see what's what in the kitchen. The girl next door said she'd make tea – though I'm perfectly capable of making it myself."

He walked stiffly out of the room, leaning quite heavily on his stick.

The 'girl' next door was at least forty-five.

"You were misinformed," Ruth said to me. "He hasn't lost his marbles, just his manners."

"Shush," I said, hurrying away from the open door towards a fireside sofa, hoping she'd follow me. "He might hear you."

"I don't care if he does," said Ruth. But she did follow me and sit down.

"Well I do! He's a client and we have to be polite to him."

"Are you *sure* you've got this right?" said Ruth. "Are you *sure* you have to be polite to them even when they insult you?"

"It goes with the job – you know that."

"Well I can't do it," said Ruth. "I can't and that's that."

"You don't have to. Just keep quiet while I simper."

41

"How can I possibly keep quiet," said Ruth, "if you're going to *simper*? It'll be enough to make a maggot throw up!"

Fine, I thought, I see what happens now. I have to be strong enough to keep Ruth under control, weak enough to convince Mr M I'm on the level, and also pretend I have a meaningful relationship with a virtual stranger. I wonder if I'll ever get my own personality back again.

"So what do you do? College? Work?" Mr Mitchell asked rather accusingly, as soon as the four of us were sitting around holding mugs. The tea was so strong it made my teeth feel furry.

"I work for my parents," I said. I had decided to keep my answers brief, and as truthful as possible.

"What do they do?" said Mrs Frost, politely interested.

"Run a travel agency."

Mr Mitchell leaned forward and frowned at me. "So what's all this about being scared of a simple journey?" he said. "You must be used to travel."

Ha, I thought, can't catch me like that.

"My parents have never taken me on business trips," I said truthfully, "because trips like that are all meetings and no sightseeing. And we don't go abroad on holidays often because that's too much like work to them."

"Hm," said Mr Mitchell. He leant back in his chair, but he was still staring at me very intently. "I'll make a bargain with you. Okay?"

"Well . . ." I stuttered.

"I will escort you to Oz," he said. "In return, when we get there, you will help out with a little scenario I have in mind."

I stared at him.

"All right?" he said sharply.

"Well . . ." I began again.

"Good," he said. "We understand each other."

Before I had time to say that I didn't think we did, he went on.

"I don't care to ask my family," he said. "My nieces never listen to a word I say, and anyway they'd probably tell me it was illegal or something."

Just at that rather tense moment the doorbell rang. Ruth said later she thought she'd have to scrape me off the ceiling. It wasn't that bad, but I did jump.

Mrs Frost began to get to her feet, but Mr Mitchell stopped her. He was actually smiling. "It could be them," he said, heaving himself to his feet and setting off for the door at quite a good speed.

Mrs Frost relaxed back into her chair. "He thinks it might be the Hallowe'en Trick-or-Treaters," she said.

"So what's he going to do to them?" said Ruth, as he disappeared into the hall. "Beat them off with his stick?"

"Oh no!" said Mrs Frost, looking shocked. "Didn't you see the pumpkin head in the hall?"

We looked blank.

"He's hollowed out a pumpkin – given it eyes and a grin and everything," said Mrs Frost, "and filled it with sweets. He did that last year as well but no one came." She tapped the side of her nose conspiratorially. "This year I put the word about," she said. "I'm just hoping it worked."

We listened as the front door was opened. We heard the high, squeaky voices. We heard the thank yous from the accompanying adult. We watched as

43

Mr Mitchell made his way back into the room and across to his chair, beaming to himself. It was quite obvious it *had* worked.

Then he looked across at us again and the smile went. "I like it here," he said tersely. "I don't want to be shipped out to the Sydney suburbs!"

Mrs Frost began to say something polite about being sure he'd be glad to see old haunts and old faces again, but he interrupted her.

"So how did you meet Tom," he said, glowering at me, "if you never go anywhere?"

The question took me completely by surprise and I hesitated.

"Tom came to Europe," said Ruth rapidly. "You remember?"

Her attitude had changed completely. She was looking at him with respect and even a bit of affection. This was a man who understood how to behave on Hallowe'en. She was obviously willing to forgive him a lot for that.

I didn't have time to feel relieved that she'd stopped being hostile. I was too busy worrying about the possibly illegal favour he seemed to expect.

"Yes," said Mr Mitchell slowly, "he did come here, didn't he? He came with my nieces. Remind me which one is his mother?"

"Neither," said Mrs Frost. "They're his aunts. Their brother is his father."

"That'll be right," said Mr Mitchell. "So he's my great-nephew then?"

That was when Ruth realised that Tom's great-uncle knew rather less about him than we did. That was also when she began to prattle enthusiastically –

to cheer him up, she explained afterwards – inventing Tom as she went along.

Dazed, I listened to tales of Tom's surfing abilities, his swimming medals, his interest in Renaissance art and his enthusiasm for fish. She was unstoppable – mainly because I couldn't think of any other topic of conversation.

I know it's a good idea to live for the moment, but sometimes it's wise to be aware of other moments, too – in this case, the moment when Mitch would inevitably meet Tom again and discover the truth. Whatever that was.

I didn't know which was harder to deal with – Ruth in contrary mode or Ruth deciding a crabby old man was Santa Claus in his rest-of-the-year clothes.

"You seem to know more about him than Jo," said Mr Mitchell eventually.

"Oh," said Ruth hastily, "I only know what Jo told me."

"Perhaps he's wise to fall for an English girl," said Mr Mitchell, suddenly wistful. "I married an English girl myself. Much more faithful than Australian girls – until she went and died, of course."

Not hostile to English girls, then, I thought. The Power Women certainly didn't seem to have listened to him.

"Met a girl in Sydney when I was young," he went on, more or less to himself. "Went on a trip into the bush and when I got back she was not only married, she had a child as well!"

"How long were you away?" said Ruth.

"Only three or four years."

"Had you asked her to wait for you?" I said cautiously.

He snorted. "Shouldn't have had to," he said. "Shouldn't have to tell women all that stuff about loving them. Should know without being told."

"Maybe she thought you weren't coming back," said Ruth.

"Why would she think that? We had an understanding. Don't see why things should be any different just because I went bush. I've never changed – the war didn't change me – living in England hasn't changed me. Some things should never change."

"Most things do, though," said Ruth. She seemed to have cast herself in the role of psychological adviser. "You'll find Sydney very different from when you knew it, I expect."

"Everything'll look older," said Mr Mitchell. "But I look older myself, so that's fair enough." He heaved a huge sigh. "You'd think," he said, "that given my age those nieces of mine might have arranged for a companion to look after *me*. Instead of expecting me to be responsible for some nervous girl."

There was a tiny startled pause.

Ruth said hastily, "I'm sure you'll be able to help each other." Then she encouraged him to tell his war stories.

He'd mellowed a lot by the time we left. Ruth was very pleased with herself.

"See," she said, as I drove us home past windows decorated with bats and cobwebs, "I *can* be nice to your clients. Poor old guy. I think he enjoyed his tea party."

"You certainly changed your opinion of him fast!"

"I have an open mind," said Ruth. "I thought he was a pain at first – then I understood that he just has a strong personality. Think of him hollowing out that pumpkin! That's really sweet."

"And you did a brilliant job of inventing Tom," I said acidly.

"Yup," said Ruth smugly. "And you hardly said anything so he thinks you're a total dweeb, which is what you wanted. What a team we are!"

A pumpkin-head jack-o-lantern leered at me from the top of someone's gatepost.

"But we don't go on being a team, do we?" I said. "You realise I now have to try and remember everything you said all through a twenty-five hour trek!"

"Shoot!" said Ruth, sitting bolt upright and almost strangling herself with her seat-belt. "I'd kind of forgotten you were off on a solo flight!"

"Also – what happens when he meets up with Tom again and discovers that what you said – and I agreed with – is all wrong?"

"He'll have forgotten by then," said Ruth. "You can tell he has memory lapses. He'll have forgotten. Won't he?"

"And if he hasn't?"

"Tom'll have to keep up the pretence. I didn't say anything outrageous."

"That could work," I said. "But what I'd like you to do now, *team*-mate, is remind me of all the stuff you told Mr M. If we run through it two or three times I'll be able to remember it."

"You think *I* can remember it?" said Ruth. "I have memory lapses, too, you know."

"Terrific! And what about this sinister scenario I'm supposed to help him with. I get the horrible feeling he thinks I agreed."

"He was just teasing," said Ruth. "I bet he doesn't have any kind of scenario in mind – certainly not a weird one."

"I'd like to believe you," I said. "I wonder if you're right."

"I am totally right," said Ruth with absolute conviction.

Anybody but me would have guessed at once that she was totally wrong.

CHAPTER SEVEN

. . . *Your Flight is now Boarding* . . .

Ruth came to Heathrow to see me off. Mr Mitchell, of course, was convinced she was there to see *him* off. I didn't argue.

I arrived dazed by lack of sleep because I'd had to get up so early. I'd done my last minute bag-check in my bedroom with my eyes only half open and darkness pressing against the windows from outside.

Ruth's brilliant plan had played havoc with my packing. I now needed clothes for an Australian spring *and* an American winter. I'd abandoned any hope of travelling light.

I'd also dropped my passport behind the bed twice, lost my ticket down the side of my case once, and knocked the bedside lamp over with the shoulder strap of my hand-luggage. For my finale, I'd managed to cut my finger on the edge of my address book and bleed all the way from L to R.

The reason for all this agony was that check-in time was more or less at dawn. It always seems to be, whenever I go anywhere. I wonder if anyone ever takes off at a reasonable time of day. And if anyone does, I wonder why it's never me.

What made things worse this time was that Dad

had driven me to Heathrow the long way, via Mr Mitchell's house, which meant we'd had to allow an extra hour or more.

Mr Mitchell, who said we were to call him Mitch, was as subdued as I was. For him, though, it was more than just being tired because he'd had to eat breakfast in the middle of the night. He must have felt really strange about going home after all those years.

I was sorry if he was suffering, but I couldn't help liking it better when he was quiet.

By the time we met up with Ruth, who'd dragged herself and her luggage in by tube, I already felt as if I'd lived through a whole day.

Ruth had luggage with her because she was flying to America on the same date. We'd discovered this more or less at the last minute. The way Ruth's father plays it is that he makes a general arrangement with her about what time of year she's to visit. Then suddenly her tickets arrive in the post and she starts to pack.

She has mentioned to him that a short postal delay could mean her plane would leave without her and she wouldn't even know she'd missed it. This has no effect. Ruth says her father has never been very comfortable with forward-planning.

Dad had found us a table in the cafeteria and bought four coffees and four Danish pastries. He and Mitch struggled bravely with a conversation about cricket. This gave Ruth a chance to tell me privately that all I had to do was relax and enjoy myself for the next week. I promised I'd try.

"My journey time's a lot shorter than yours," she said thoughtfully, "so I'll arrive first. Won't I? Except that I leave later. And Sydney time's ahead of UK *and* USA time. You're flying into the future! Maybe that means you'll arrive first. By some clock or other. Do you think?"

"I can't stand it," I said. "Working out time differences scrambles my brains. I just know I reach Sydney tomorrow night."

"Call me from Sydney," said Ruth. "Here's my father's number – and this one's the fax."

"Oh yes," I said, "I'm really likely to fax the USA from Mrs Cooper's house, aren't I? And it'd cost a fortune to ring."

"That's okay. They're rich."

"Sh!" I said, glancing across the table at Mitch.

"He's not listening," said Ruth. "Anyway I'm talking quietly. I do have *some* social graces."

"Yes, well, I don't want them to think I'm taking advantage of them."

"They won't. Anyway, they're taking advantage of you, hauling you half-way around the universe because it suits them. The fact that it happens to suit you too is beside the point. They don't know that."

"I'll play it by ear," I said.

"That's what telephoning's all about," said Ruth smugly.

I couldn't be irritated with her. Coming to see me off was an act of true friendship. Her flight wasn't due out until seven hours after ours.

In fact everyone had been so especially nice to me that I had begun to wonder if they knew something – like that the plane was destined to drop into the ocean from 10,000 feet, for instance.

George had even lent me his lucky key ring. You might think this was not especially generous since

George doesn't have any keys, but he really likes that ring. Or anyway he really likes the metal skull with the hinged jaw that hangs from it.

My mother, who'd been faxed in Spain with the news, had sent me details of the agent the company deals with in Sydney. She'd said she'd like me to call in on her and say hello. She'd added that it never does any harm to remind people that Quest exists, and that it's effective and efficient. I liked that.

Peggy tried to give me some spending money, the way she did when I went to Paris. This time I didn't let her. Peggy is almost like an honorary aunt, so I wasn't offended. All the same, taking it would have made me feel like a schoolgirl.

Bill gave me a few useful tips about Australia, and added, "The girls dress up a bit in the evening, but you can be quite casual in the daytime." Typical of Bill to know that.

Gone are the days when he never, for any reason, bothered to look at me. Now he looks – but never flirts. In fact it's quite possible that I'm the only living human female he doesn't flirt with – if you exclude his mother.

At first Ruth said it's because he respects me too much. I didn't find that convincing. So then she said it's because he respects my parents too much. I can just about go along with that. If I work at it.

"I think you and Mitch had better get moving," said my father, stacking all the coffee cups in a determined way.

"What will you do with yourself till you can check in?" I said to Ruth.

"Spend too much in the airport shops, eat too much in the airport cafeteria, mulch around dumping my bag where people'll fall over it and try not to get arrested. The usual stuff."

Then she pulled me a little away from the other two. "Does Tom plan to be at Sydney airport to meet you?" she said.

"I don't know. I only know Mrs Cooper's going to be there."

"Right, but don't forget, if Tom is there, and if Mitch is watching, you have to greet him as if you're pleased to see him. I mean, *really* pleased to see him."

I didn't spot the elegant Marina until after the flight had been called. Then, as Mitch and I made our slow and dignified progress along the canvas tube that funnels you directly onto the plane, I noticed her. She was well ahead of us, walking briskly, swinging an Italian designer bag. How do I know it was an Italian designer bag? I don't, but I'm sure it was.

Even then, with Mitch beside me and her ahead, the only thing on my mind was that final remark of Ruth's. I had completely forgotten that, for the next several hours, my main problem was likely to be my travelling companions.

CHAPTER EIGHT

A Desperate Man

I was extremely glad to get back on the plane at the end of our short stop in Thailand. After a thirteen-hour flight, you might think I'd have had enough of it, but at least on the plane Mitch was under control.

He'd eaten meals, stared at the films and sitcoms on the screen up-front, read the in-flight magazine, slept. I'd done the same and had decided that this was not such a tough assignment after all.

Mitch on the loose in Don Muang Airport, though, was a nightmare – mainly because he refused to believe that the most we were ever going to see of Bangkok was the transit lounge.

Also I spent a lot of energy trying to avoid Marina. Don't misunderstand me. I like Marina. I really do. Marina is a nice person. It's just that I didn't see how I could impress her with my cool efficiency while at the same time pretending to be a kid-on-holiday for the benefit of Mitch.

I felt I could cope with either of them separately, but not with both of them together. Especially as Mitch refused to take me seriously. Even when I said, "Mr Mitchell, transit passengers are *never* allowed out of the airport."

"How many times do I have to tell you to call me Mitch? Are you deaf or daft?"

The silly thing was I'd been calling him Mitch in my own mind for hours. For some reason I just found it difficult to say it aloud.

"Sorry," I said, "Mitch! Whatever I call you, you still can't go out of the transit lounge."

"I know about these things and you don't. I've been to Bangkok three times over the years, and I've *always* visited the Grand Palace and the Temple of the Emerald Buddha!"

I kept glancing around the crowded transit lounge, but I couldn't see Marina. I convinced myself that she'd only been travelling as far as Bangkok. That meant she would have been shunted through different doors. Possibly she was, even now, training her luminous eyes on the Emerald Buddha.

Then I spotted her – calm, collected and uncrushed – over by the bar.

"Let's go this way," I said to Mitch, leaning against his arm and aiming him in the opposite direction.

"You have to understand that you are my responsibility," said Mitch, more or less walking where I was pushing him. "That means I don't just have to keep you safe, I have to show you interesting things as well."

I was touched by that. I felt a warm glow of something like affection.

"It's okay," I said, looking around for something in the transit lounge that might get his attention. "There's lots to see here."

"Like what!" said Mitch. "Airport shops are the same the world over."

"These smell different. Also they have more

orchids," I said. "Really, I don't *want* to go sight-seeing."

"That's because you're too ignorant to know what you're missing," said Mitch sharply.

My warm glow cooled down.

"Listen," I said, in my pleading voice, "we only have just over two hours here. There wouldn't be time anyway."

"Certainly there would. A cab to the centre only takes forty minutes."

"You'd be lucky, mate," said a passing traveller, with a heavy Australian accent. "More like ninety. On a good day."

It was at that moment, when I was distracted by the possibility that Mitch might believe the unknown traveller even if he didn't believe me, that we finally bumped into Marina. Almost literally. She had obviously decided to leave the bar and take some exercise.

She and I both did the 'goodness, fancy seeing you here' stuff. Then I introduced her to Mitch.

Of course she was charming to him, of course Mitch was dazzled, and of course the first thing he said to her was, "Jo is not used to travelling alone so I am taking care of her."

For one second I was tempted to give the game away. Fortunately, the second passed.

Marina looked at me with an amused smile. Then she said to Mitch, "I'm sure you're an excellent courier. I know it isn't an easy task."

I smiled weakly at no one in particular.

"She's frightened of everything, that's the problem," said Mitch, as if I wasn't there. "Won't take any risks."

"Oh dear," said Marina. Her smile was broader. If

she wasn't so infuriatingly poised, I think she might have laughed aloud.

"Keeps insisting we can't go sightseeing," said Mitch.

"It's possible she might be right about that," said Marina. "I believe that is the rule."

"No worries," said Mitch. "I like to beat the system."

My self-image was so crushed by now that I hardly had the energy to worry about that.

Marina excused herself and drifted off. Mitch and I continued our hunt for the exit. At least, Mitch hunted and I kept pace. He wasn't fast, but he was determined. Despite my best efforts to steer him the wrong side of a flower stall, he succeeded in spotting the door that connected with the rest of the airport.

He stomped off towards it looking very much as though he might use his stick to force his way through.

I followed, getting more agitated by the second. I was terrified he'd succeed in getting out, and then of course I'd have to go with him.

I didn't know exactly what would happen next – whether we'd get lost or abducted or just stuck in a traffic jam – but I was certain we'd miss the flight. I tried not to imagine Mrs Cooper's reaction when our luggage arrived in Sydney without us.

It turned out we were a whole lot safer than I'd thought. All the passengers who were joining the flight at Bangkok were busily filing in at the door Mitch was hoping to file out at.

What was more, an airline official in a nifty uniform was checking their boarding passes. Mitch, on his ferocious bid for freedom, found his path firmly blocked.

There is something about airline officials. They can be very nice, very smooth, very helpful. They can also be extremely firm. Even Mitch had to give way.

Not before he'd insisted we do a circuit of the lounge twice, though. "If we can just come up on his blind side," he'd said, "and take him by surprise, we'll make it."

After the third try I pointed out that we were down to less than an hour now, and nothing short of sonic roller-blades could get us into town and back again in time.

For once, he agreed with me. We found two seats and sank into them. He didn't speak. I watched him anxiously, afraid he might be hatching some subversive plot. Then I realised he was simply worn out.

I risked leaving him to go to the Ladies. That's when I saw Marina for the third and final time.

She turned round from the mirror, gave me a radiant smile, and said, "He must be quite a handful. Brilliant idea to let him think he's looking after you."

I could have hugged her. My self-image straightened itself out and dusted itself down. I managed a fairly radiant smile myself.

By the time we parted, even I had to accept that Marina regarded me as a colleague and an equal. Somewhere inside my head I seemed to hear Ruth saying, "Well of course she does, you bozo, what did you think?"

Even so, I freely admit I didn't specially want to be in Marina's shadow when Tom was around.

I've never wanted to be able to see the whole of my future, in case I didn't like it. But sometimes it would be nice to be able to see bits. If I could have known that not only would I not see Marina again as we got off the plane, but also that I wouldn't bump into her in Sydney either, I wouldn't have spent the week looking over my shoulder.

Mitch didn't start talking again till we were airborne. Then he let rip. I swear that the nearer we got to Sydney, the more Australian he sounded and the weirder his stories became.

First he had a go at the Power Women. He said they liked to think they were superior, but *he'd* show them. "My family are all snobs," he said. "Don't look so surprised. Aussies can be just as snobby as Poms!"

Then he talked about the Missing Years, the years when he went off into the bush, and when the girl he'd left behind married someone else.

"I thought my Missing Years were the best years of my life," he said wistfully, "until I got back."

He said he'd done all sorts of jobs in the Missing Years, including studying numbats in the field.

"You mean wombats?" I said, to show I did know something about Australian wildlife.

He just glared at me and said he knew what he meant.

I didn't want to annoy him, so when he said he'd spent six months organising camel races, I didn't point out that camels come from Asia and North Africa, not Australia.

Suddenly he began to talk about his father. "We were always fighting," he said cheerfully. "Too alike, probably. You won't believe this, but in my youth I was quite wild."

Funnily enough, I did believe that.

"We had such rows," he said dreamily. "Especially after my mother died."

I remembered what Mrs Cooper had told me. "Then you had a really big fight and left the country, didn't you?" I said.

Mitch smiled to himself. "I left the country because of the biggest fight of all," he said.

"And you've really never been back?"

"I buried the past and walked away," said Mitch. "In fact you'd be surprised what I buried!" Then he said something that didn't sound odd at first. "When I get back, I plan to reclaim my inheritance from my father."

It didn't sound odd because I thought he meant his inheritance had been left to him by his father, and that he was going to reclaim it from a lawyer or someone. But when I asked politely who was looking after it, he gave rather a peculiar laugh and said his father was.

Then it did sound odd. I began to feel edgy.

"Do you get on with *your* father?" he said. "Even though he never takes you on holidays?"

"We do things together," I said, thinking I saw a chance to get him onto a more normal subject. "We go bird-watching sometimes."

Mitch snorted. "English birds! Things that tweet on twigs and peck at crumbs. In Australia we have a bird that swallows huge fruits whole. Then it eats stones and jumps up and down until they mash the fruit into a pulp in its stomach. That's a *real* bird for you."

I thought it was best not to say anything.

"You get much tougher, wilder breeds in Australia," he went on. "What's London famous for? Pigeons! Sydney has flying foxes!"

He didn't seem to be mad, but then who was I to judge?

"Ever been shrimping in England?" he said, clearly not ready to give up on the zoology fantasy yet.

"When I was very young," I said warily.

"And how did the shrimps behave?" said Mitch.

"What do you mean?"

"I bet they just scuttled about hiding under rocks," said Mitch. "In Australia, shrimps are armed! They shoot people who come after them."

I laughed. Not because I thought it was funny, but to check if he was joking. He wasn't.

"They don't use bullets, of course," said Mitch.

"Oh?" I think I managed to sound politely surprised.

"No! Water pistols!"

I was tempted to ask if the koalas were issued with kalashnikovs, but decided not to push it.

Suddenly Mitch swivelled right round in his seat and peered at me anxiously. "Once we get to Sydney," he said, "I have to clear up an important bit of my past. I may not be able to manage by myself. I can rely on you, can't I?"

For the second time I seemed to hear Ruth's voice in my head. This time she said, "The man is insane but harmless. Be nice to him and don't worry."

Mildly comforted, I said primly that it depended what he wanted me to do.

"Doesn't depend on anything," said Mitch. "You made a promise to help. I'm holding you to it."

"No," I said firmly. "You asked me to promise but I didn't. I *knew* you weren't listening to me."

"My nieces do that," said Mitch.

"Do what?" I said, totally confused.

"Not listen," said Mitch. He sank back in his seat. I began to relax. It had been very alarming, being stared at with his fierce blue eyes.

Naturally, relaxing was a mistake.

"I'm not letting you off," he said. "We had a deal."

I began to speak, but he talked on regardless.

"If you let me down," he said, "I shall tell Tom that you embarrassed me on the trip by flirting outrageously with every man you saw!"

"But that wouldn't be true!" I said.

"I could make him believe it."

"That wouldn't be fair!" I said. I may have said it quite loudly.

He shrugged, closed his eyes and settled himself more comfortably. "I never pretended to be a fair man," he said, in the slightly mumbly tones of someone who is just dropping off to sleep. "I'm a desperate man."

I'd be lying if I said that didn't make me uneasy. Even so, I still managed to reassure myself. After all, everything he'd said on the second half of the flight had been weird. Yet somehow, I still didn't really believe he was off his head. So the answer had to be that he was teasing me – which was what Ruth had said after the tea party.

"It's okay," I said more calmly. "I don't mind you pulling my leg."

Mitch didn't answer. At least, not in words. He just chuckled.

I can't explain why, but it was the most unnerving chuckle I've ever heard in my life.

CHAPTER NINE

The Reunion

There are moments in life that are designed to humiliate you for as long as you remember them. Sometimes you can't see them coming. Sometimes you can see them coming and think you can avoid them, but they get you anyway.

As Mitch and I pushed our luggage trolley out into the main concourse at Kingsford-Smith Airport, I was fairly calm. My only slight anxiety was that I might not recognise Tom.

However, I had quite decided how I was going to greet him. I was going to be friendly but distant. I was going to behave exactly as I had when I'd met Marina. And I would watch his reaction. That way I'd find out if he really liked me or not. I'd always had this sneaky feeling that it might be Ruth he liked. It's true he sent me two postcards from Europe, but maybe he'd got our names mixed up. Maybe it was Ruth he was expecting to see right now!

Maybe he wasn't even *at* the Airport.

Two seconds later I discovered that he definitely was at the Airport and that I definitely did recognise him.

I'd *entirely* forgotten how extraordinarily good-looking he is.

Mrs Cooper was right beside him. I'd *entirely* forgotten how extremely forceful she is.

In her familiar, loud, power woman's voice she called out, "Uncle Mitch! Welcome! And thank you for riding shotgun with Tom's young lady."

Then, ignoring the fact that Tom is so much bigger than she is, she gave him a shove in my direction that actually made him stagger.

At exactly the same moment, Mitch nudged me out from behind the trolley so that Tom and I were not more than two feet apart.

Fat chance of guessing at Tom's real feelings with the olds being about as sensitive as a pair of runaway tanks.

It was like that scene in a film where a couple face each other and the music plays and everyone else goes out of focus. The problem was that we both went out of focus, too.

Tom was definitely more relaxed than I was, but only just. He said, "Hi, great to see you." Then he swayed towards me with his hands out to catch me by the shoulders. As soon as he had hold of me, he bent down.

It was obvious he was planning to kiss me on the cheek. A good compromise and quite convincing enough for Mitch, this being a public place and all.

I tried to co-operate, I really did. But we were both moving fast, keen to get this bit over with, and Tom is a lot taller than I am, and we'd never been this close before. Between us we made a total mess of it.

What I was meant to get was a brief hug and a peck on the cheek. What I actually got was Tom treading heavily on my right foot and jabbing his nose hard into my left eye. It's surprising how rapidly pain destroys romance.

As I staggered back, my face bright red and my eye watering, I caught sight of Mrs Cooper watching us. She was not wearing a nice expression. I swear she was enjoying my embarrassment.

Now that her uncle was safely in Sydney she'd probably realised that there had never been any need for me to fly with him. Like Ruth had said, my fare had been paid for by a guilty conscience. And now she didn't mind at all if I had to suffer for my free holiday.

I had an almost overwhelming urge to say, "Hey, Mitch, she lied to you! It's all a set-up! *I'm* the escort!" I overcame it, though. Mrs Cooper was the client. I owed it to Quest to go along with what she wanted. Unfortunately.

The ride to her house was a nightmare. She drove like you'd think she would, fast and pushily. I felt sleepy and sick and – even though I'd changed my clothes on the flight – much too hot. Also my eye was still watering. I avoided looking at Tom, so I don't know if his nose was red.

He and I sat silently in the back. Mitch, who must have been exhausted by now, sat silently in the front. Mrs Cooper, who doesn't go in for being silent, kept up a running commentary about the wonders of Sydney.

Sydney, which was all stuffy darkness and brilliant lights, looked large and confusing.

I was extremely glad when we arrived at the house. I might not have behaved with Marina's poise, but at least I hadn't thrown up.

Although it was late when we got in, the table was laid and Mrs Cooper told us to sit down. Then she hurried into the kitchen. Tom and Mitch sat down immediately, opposite each other. I sat beside Mitch.

The house – or anyway the bit I could see from where I was sitting – looked very opulent. I decided Mum could have organised an entire Quest for Antiques Tour in the sitting-room alone.

Mitch craned his neck towards the kitchen. This was obviously male-code for something. Tom understood it at once.

"You want a beer?" he said. "Sure," and he got up and fetched one.

I couldn't decide if he was deliberately avoiding talking to me, or if he was just being nice to his great-uncle.

Before I had time to worry much about that, Mrs Cooper came back in with some dishes on a tray, announcing, "Dinner!"

It was the sort of dinner someone might make you go to as a punishment if you'd annoyed them. I mean *really* annoyed them.

We had rice and a huge bowl of seafood stew.

I could see at once that nothing had been shelled before it had been cooked. I think she'd simply boiled a rockpool. Eating the occasional prawn is one thing. Being faced with an entire shoal of the things – armed or not – is another. I've never quite got round to being a vegetarian, but there was something about the clusters of pink feelers wavering about above the gravy that made me wonder if this might be the time to start.

Mrs Cooper dumped a ladleful on each plate and left us to sort it out from there.

There was an empty pot on the table for all the surplus claws and shells and whiskery bits. As it filled up it began to look unnervingly similar to the pot we were eating from.

The best I could say for it was that it gave us all something to do, to take our minds off the awkward conversation.

I don't know why, but the mussels were the worst. Their shells were slightly open so I could see what looked like tiny bits of clammy shrivelled brain inside. Quite a lot of them had clattered onto my plate and I knew – I just knew – that it wasn't done to refuse any part of Mrs Cooper's feast. Apart from anything else, it was supposed to be a treat.

I managed a few shrimps, and one or two unknown rubbery things, and all the time the mussel-shells were grating reproachfully against each other, reminding me that I still had to face up to them.

By now Mitch was talking about his Missing Years and Mrs Cooper was telling him that he hadn't been out in the bush at all. "I may have been a child at the time," she said, "but I remember the stories. You spent those years in Melbourne, working in an office." Then she added under her breath, "And getting into debt." I don't think I was meant to hear that bit.

I felt sorry for Mitch. Even though I'd suspected he was making up all those stories on the plane, I didn't see why she couldn't go along with it.

He didn't mind though. He just laughed. "Ha!" he said, "that's what I told the family to annoy them because *they* all wanted to live in posh Melbourne. I went bush, all right, but that's all over. Now it's my turn to be posh. I plan to buy a nice house and employ a housekeeper. I shall probably invite you all over sometimes."

That was when I made the wonderful discovery that if I just fiddled with a mussel and then flung the whole thing into the rubbish pot, everyone assumed I'd eaten it.

"Now, Mitch," said Mrs Cooper, "we have everything settled . . ."

"I'm sure you've got me a billet in a most charming retirement home," said Mitch. "But hard luck, you'll have to cancel. I plan to be independent."

"Well there's no need to talk about it now," said Mrs Cooper. She winced as my final mussel landed among the empties with a triumphant clang.

Mitch, who had enjoyed his dinner so much he'd had a second helping, waved his fork at her and said, "*You* think I won't be able to afford a nice house and a nice housekeeper. But when I get my inheritance . . ."

Unexpectedly, he swivelled round in his chair to face me and give me a huge wink.

Keep calm, I said to myself, he's afraid of having his life taken over by his power niece, that's all. He just needs to pretend he has an important secret. All I have to do is smile knowingly and he'll be happy.

I smiled knowingly.

He may have been happy, but Mrs Cooper wasn't. I caught sight of her face. She was looking decidedly rattled.

"There isn't any point talking like that," she said, and began to gather up the plates with much fuss and bustle.

"That was beaut," said Mitch, patting his stomach. "Short of crocodile snags and kangaroo steaks, you couldn't have chosen better."

I laughed nervously.

"It's true," said Tom, picking up the two bowls. "We do have croc sausages."

"Not in this house," said Mrs Cooper frostily, leading the way out to the kitchen.

As soon as she and Tom were out of earshot, Mitch leaned towards me and said conspiratorially, "They'll have to sit up and take notice once it's all sorted out!"

Mrs Cooper would be back any second. I didn't have long. "Mitch, I'd really like to get this straight," I said. "You *are* just winding her up and teasing me, aren't you?"

Mitch opened his mouth to answer, but at that moment Mrs Cooper strode back in, carrying a different bowl, and he turned his attention to her instead.

"I don't mean the inheritance *you* think I mean," he said. "Don't look so worried! I don't mean the inheritance my father left to my brother! The inheritance my brother then left to you and *your* brother and sister."

I noticed with relief that this bowl didn't have anything alarming in it. Just ice cream.

"I don't mean *that* inheritance," Mitch droned on. "I mean *my* inheritance."

"Now then, Tom," said Mrs Cooper sharply, obviously desperate to change the subject. "You're far too quiet. I'm sure your great-uncle would like to hear something about your life and interests. He has a lot of catching up to do."

"No," said Mitch, "you're all right, Tom. I've heard all about you from Ruth. You know, the redhead."

Tom knew perfectly well that Ruth knew almost nothing about him. He didn't say so, though. Just looked faintly puzzled.

"Nice girl," Mitch went on, "but now I think about it I can see why you picked this one. More peaceful. Tell me – what are your plans – where are you taking her?"

My eye had stopped watering, but somehow that made it begin again. I pretended to push my hair back and managed to wipe it discreetly.

"I'm cutting lectures tomorrow," said Tom, "to show her round Sydney."

"Good," said Mitch. "She deserves a bit of fun," he fixed me with his bright blue eyes again, "before she has to get to work for me."

"No, Mitch," said Mrs Cooper, "Jo is here for a holiday. If you need anything done, you have your family now."

Mitch shook his head, smiling rather smugly, I thought. "Jo and I have an understanding," he said.

"I think we'll all understand each other better," said Mrs Cooper, "after a good night's sleep."

I thought that was unlikely, but I was willing to give it a try. In fact, given the choice, I'd have gone to bed as soon as we got in, but no one had shown me where my room was, and I hadn't liked to ask. I was aware that, as far as Mrs Cooper was concerned, I wasn't really supposed to be there at all.

We all got up from the table. Tom walked over and picked up my bags.

It was only then that I realised Tom was driving me over to stay at his house.

You might think that the ten minutes alone with Tom in his car would have been the perfect time to ask him straight out how he really felt about my visit. I didn't, though. I knew he was far too nice to say anything nasty, so anything he *did* say would have been meaningless.

Also I was more tired than I think I've ever been before. So I sat quietly and pretended the set-up really was as cosy as it must have looked from outside the car. Just the two of us, driving home together after an evening out.

Tom seemed perfectly relaxed, but still not in talking mode. The silence was peaceful rather than unfriendly, but it still worried me. The trouble with silent people is you never know what's going on in their heads.

By the time we were pulling up outside another nice house in another nice suburb, I was beginning to think that if I didn't say something soon, neither of us would ever speak again.

"By the way," I began. The sound of my voice made us both jump. "I'm afraid Ruth got a bit carried away when she met Mitch back in England. She sort of 'invented' you."

"Oh?" said Tom. "I hope I turned out nice?"

He didn't wait for an answer, but got out of the car and began to drag my cases out of the back.

I looked up at the house and saw curtains twitching at the front windows and a couple watching us unload.

It suddenly seemed worse than I'd thought. One minute Tom was someone I'd exchanged about seven sentences with on a Paris street. The next I was on the other side of the world living in his parents' house. It was all too sudden.

Still, at least I wasn't living in Mrs Cooper's house,

as I'd expected. At least I was well away from Mitch. If he really did have strange plans in mind, he'd just have to sort them out without me.

Or so I thought.

CHAPTER TEN

A Date with Sydney Harbour

My first day started out all right – even though I woke up wondering where I was. I looked round the pretty bedroom. I screwed up my eyes against the sun which was trying to shine through the curtains. I listened to birds I'd never heard before singing outside.

Then I remembered. I'd made it. I was in Sydney.

I looked at my watch, which was on local time. It was almost two in the afternoon. I crept out of my room to an empty house. I guessed everyone was out at work or school or college.

When I'd washed and dressed, I went into the kitchen area. There was a note on the counter which said, 'I'll be back later to take you to the Harbour – Tom'. There was a note on the fridge in different writing that said 'Help yourself to brekkie.' There was a home-made card with a picture of a kangaroo on it that said, 'Jo – Welcome to Oz – love from Melanie.'

I couldn't believe how nice these people were. After all, Tom's father was the power women's brother. You'd think he'd be as pushy as his sisters. He wasn't, though, he was as laid-back as Tom. I wondered if it had anything to do with the fact that, unlike them, he's not rich. Or was I just being prejudiced?

I'd discovered that I really liked both Tom's parents, *and* his kid sister Melanie. It had also been a huge relief to find they were in on Mrs Cooper's tall story. They knew I was a courier – they knew I wasn't Tom's girl. I could be myself with them.

I could tell they liked me too. I'd decided that even Tom liked me. But, unfortunately, only in the way his parents and his sister did.

Amazing how twenty-odd hours shut in a metal capsule, breathing stale air and eating unreal food, can temporarily blind a person to the totally obvious. Now that I wasn't tired any more I could understand the situation very well. If Tom had been really pleased to have me around for a week – I mean *really* pleased the way Ruth (and I) had hoped – he'd have said so. It was as simple as that. Or so it seemed to me.

Still, there was no reason why we couldn't have a nice time together. We didn't need to pretend we were dating now Mitch wasn't around.

The important thing, I decided, was to make it obvious that I wasn't expecting anything more than a casual friendship. It would be awful if Tom thought I'd misunderstood. What if he decided he had to break it to me that I wasn't his type or something!

So I planned to be polite and cheerful – but aloof. Kind of formal. I thought that would reassure him that I hadn't read anything into the hideously botched kiss the night before.

If I played it right then maybe, just maybe, the sightseeing trip would subtly turn into a date and take us both by surprise.

Playing it right wasn't so easy, though. I talked too much. Two things make me do that – being nervous and being with someone who hardly talks at all. So it wasn't entirely my fault.

I prattled all the way to the station, all the way in on the train, and all the way through the crowds of sightseers and backpackers to the dock where we got the harbour boat.

I think I only stopped once, when I was briefly distracted by a bull terrier in a tee-shirt with pink sunblock on its nose.

"That's extraordinary!" I said.

Tom looked where I was looking. "Yeah," he said, "with white dogs they usually put block on the ears as well." It was one of his longest sentences.

The harbour was unexpectedly enormous and seemed to get bigger as the boat carried us around. It wasn't just a harbour, it was a sea, with inlets and headlands and islands. And it was so busy! I think I'd expected the yachts and windsurfers, but there was heavy-duty stuff as well. Not just ferries and paddle steamers but freighters and a naval frigate. The bridge was so huge it was almost scary looking up at it from underneath. And the Opera House from water-level looks even more extraordinary than it does in all those aerial shots you see.

The sun was hot, the wind was steady, the waves sloshed against the bows. I'd like to say the whole thing took my breath away, but it can't have because I heard my voice going on.

When I look back I can see there were two parallel sightseeing trips – my fantasy one and the real one.

I said: "I look that way and I see skyscrapers, I look the other way and I see palm trees, and it looks as though there's a whole town on that shore over there. This harbour is *vast*."

Fantasy-Tom replied, "I love your enthusiasm. It's a real pleasure to show you around."

Real-Tom replied, "Yup, it's big."

I said, "I've never seen the Opera House from this angle before – it looks like a prehistoric lizard creeping down to the water to drink."

Fantasy-Tom replied, "You have such an unusual and interesting way of looking at things."

Real-Tom replied, "Yup, everyone says that."

It was a bit discouraging.

Even so, Tom was actually not a bad guide. He knew the name of every harbour within the harbour, every landmark around its edges. When I'd finally worn myself out and stopped, he got his chance.

He waved his arms at the cluster of skyscrapers. "Central Business District," he said, "known as CBD." He pointed out the gold-topped Sydney Tower. "Tallest building in the Southern Hemisphere." He made sure I saw first one and then another olde-worlde sailing ship. "Working replicas of Cook's Endeavour and the Bounty."

"That was brilliant," I said as we left the boat.

"Good!" said Tom. He grinned. He might not say a lot, but he did smile. Maybe we were getting on better than it seemed.

"So what now?" he said. "You want to find somewhere with a view and sit and have a smoothie?"

"A what?"

"Sorry – milkshake to you. I recommend the banana and butterscotch but the chocolate mint thickshake is ace, too."

That sounded good to me, but on the other hand,

if we just sat and had a drink, I knew I'd go on yapping. And if I talked too much for long enough I was sure to say something stupid.

It was fairly clear to me that this was not subtly turning into a date. Or if it was, it was doing it so subtly that neither of us was aware of it.

Then I had a brainwave. If Tom *had* liked me in Paris, it had been because I was being effective and business-like. All right, so I would be effective and business-like here. It was worth a try.

"I need to call in at a travel agent Quest has dealings with," I said. "Would you mind . . .?"

"No worries," said Tom.

It was only when we got there that I realised it might not have been such a great idea after all. I'd been prepared for no one to have time to see me. I'd even been prepared for no one to have heard of Quest. I hadn't been prepared for Shelley.

Shelley had time, Shelley had heard of Quest, in fact Shelley was Quest's principal contact in Australia. She was very relaxed. She was also very friendly and very pretty. And she couldn't keep her eyes off Tom.

She gave us tea out the back, in her office. She was so relaxed, friendly (and the other thing) that she even got Tom talking.

I didn't think I was jealous. Why would I be? He wasn't mine. I thought I was perfectly calm. Or I did until I realised Shelley was asking me a question that she had obviously asked at least once before.

"Sorry?" I said.

"I was saying – would you like to call your parents from here?" said Shelley. "Let them know you've arrived safely?"

"Do you need to speak to them about anything?" I said.

"No," said Shelley, "but feel free. Though, come to think of it, it's only about seven in the morning in the UK. You might not be too popular. Like to send a fax instead?"

Something pinged in my memory.

"It's okay," I said. "They know they'd hear soon enough if anything was wrong. But I'd love to call New York, if that's all right?"

"Sure," said Shelley. She looked at her watch again, "But it's around one in the morning there. Maybe the fax is still a better idea."

"Thank you," I said. "I'll keep it to one page."

So that's how I came to leave Tom and Shelley chattering like a pair of budgerigars while I went into a cubbyhole next door and faxed Ruth.

I thought, oh well, I seem to have introduced Tom to his next girl-friend. It was only then that I realised he almost certainly had a girl-friend already. I'd been so busy being cool and remote that it hadn't occurred to me to ask him anything about his life.

I was a bit cautious about what I said in the fax. I knew that as soon as it had gone through I could tear up the original. Still I couldn't be sure that Tom wouldn't walk in any second and read it over my shoulder.

I told her about the harbour tour. That was safe and she likes water trips. I told her I was staying with Tom and his parents. That would knock her socks off. I said the flight had been fine. After that little lot I couldn't think of anything else. Or not anything I could risk Tom seeing.

So I just wrote that Mitch's scenario was getting

weirder by the minute, but that I wasn't too worried. I said I was sure she'd been right when she'd said it was a leg-pull. Especially when I thought of the other leg-pulls he'd come up with. I finished by telling her about the numbat/wombat, the stone-eating birds, the gun-slinging shrimps, and all the rest.

I didn't tell her about the intense conversation Tom still seemed to be having with Shelley in the next room. I decided not to share that with her until I was in New York.

All in all, it wasn't a great fax, but talking to Ruth always cheers me up, even if she isn't there.

We spent a bit more time with Shelley and when we left she walked with us to the door and waved us off – one wave for me and a dozen for him.

Tom and I travelled back to the eastern suburbs almost entirely in companionable silence. At least, I hoped it was companionable. Whatever – it was a relief to rest my vocal chords.

When we got back to the house, Melanie came leaping up to me to tell me I'd had a phone call from Mitch.

"You can get back to him straightaway, if you want to," said Tom's mother. "We don't eat for half an hour."

I didn't particularly want to, but it was obvious I had to.

Mitch picked up the phone instantly.

"I didn't know we wouldn't be staying in the same house," he said. "Can you get yourself over here tomorrow?"

"I'm not sure," I said.

"Can you be overheard?" said Mitch.

I was standing in the open-plan living room with

Tom's mother preparing the dinner, Tom's father opening beers, Tom's sister fiddling with the TV, and Tom threading a new lace into one of his trainers.

"Yes," I said. "Definitely."

"Right," said Mitch. "Well be careful what you say. I don't want my nieces *or* my nephew to know what I'm up to till it's all done. And it has to be done while you're still here to help me. How long do we have?"

"A few days," I said, wondering what I'd say if they asked why he'd rung.

I was aware of Melanie closing in. She took me by the elbow and led me firmly to my room, with the cordless phone still to my ear. Then she pushed me gently through the door and closed it on me.

"I'm okay now," I said to Mitch. "I have privacy."

"Good," said Mitch. "Be here in the morning. I'll have the necessary."

"The necessary *what*?"

He snorted with laughter. "I'm going to find my roots," he said.

"Tell me what you want me to do," I said. "That's only fair."

He laughed again, secretively, as if he were enjoying a private joke.

"Either you tell me now what you're talking about," I said firmly, "or I'm not having anything to do with it."

"Shan't," said Mitch. "It'd spoil the fun."

Now utterly convinced that he was teasing me, I said I had other plans and couldn't make it. I had really begun to like Mitch, but this long drawn-out fantasy was getting annoying.

He had one final try, saying that if I forced him to

go it alone it would be my fault if anything bad happened to him. Also that if he came a cropper it would give his family the excuse they needed to shut him away.

"Forget the sunset retirement home," he said, "they'll have me in an institution for ancient incompetents."

I refused to let myself pay attention to any of this.

"Are you going to tell me what you're talking about?" I said.

"No," said Mitch.

"Goodbye then," I said. "I hope we meet again before I go." And I hung up. I admit I had a moment's anxiety, but I shrugged it off quite easily.

Back in the sitting room I said to Melanie. "Thanks. That was very kind."

"Sure," said Melanie, "I hate phoning in public, too."

"We'll eat outside," said Tom's mother. "Do you guys want to take your drinks out? I'll call you when I need you to carry food."

Somehow Tom and I got out there first. And yes, since you ask, there were a few flies, but I can't blame them for what happened next.

I can only understand it if I remember I was still a bit tense about our relationship and still a bit flustered from talking to Mitch. It was all so quick. I made a total hash of things in about fifteen seconds.

Tom said, "So what would you like to do tomorrow?"

And I said, "It's okay. You don't have to pretend when Mitch isn't around. You don't have to spend time with me."

"Oh," said Tom. He was silent for half a second. Then he said, "Okay."

And that was it.

It had been nice being with him even when he didn't talk. Maybe if we'd given it another chance, he would have talked. I should have gone along with it. I should have let him take me out whether he wanted to or not.

Very impressive, I thought. I've refused to go along with Mitch's little game. I've refused to go along with Tom. *Now* what do I do?

CHAPTER ELEVEN

News of the Numbat

We ate dinner. We played board games with Melanie till she went to bed. Then Tom went to his room to do some studying and I watched a bit of TV with his parents and got an early night.

It's amazing what a normal evening a person can have, despite the fact that she's just obliterated a relationship before it's even begun.

What's even harder to believe is that I slept well. I was woken by Melanie, exploding into my room holding the cordless phone. She bounded across to the bed and stuffed it into my hand before I'd even had a chance to sit up properly.

"Quick!" she said. "Take it! It's for you. Long distance!"

I clapped it to my ear in a bit of a panic, thinking something must have gone wrong at home.

"Hi!" said a familiar voice. "I had to call Mrs Cooper to get your number. Boy, she doesn't change, does she? Still thinks she's Queen of the Universe."

"Ruth!"

"Yup, it's me, but not for long. My father's making me pay for this call so you're only getting three minutes. I have the kitchen timer by me – can you hear it ticking?"

"Yes! You're so clear. You sound as if you're just round the corner. I wish you were."

"So how's it going with Tom?"

"Don't ask! Badly."

"Okay, lady, well, you have about five days to get it right!"

"I don't think I can."

"Good grief! You're actually living in his house! Work at it!"

Before I had a chance to give her any details about yesterday, she talked on.

"Now," she said, "this might be important. I was bored over here with everyone at work and no one to talk to, so I decided to call Edward. Like you suggested, remember?"

"Of course I remember."

"I kind of needed an excuse, just to start me off, so I pretended I wanted to check your fax over with him. It turns out he knows a lot about animals, not just how to give rabies shots. And he says Mitch wasn't spinning you a line."

My insides did a little shimmy. "Tell me more," I said.

"Right – well there really is something called a numbat. It's about the size of a squirrel, long pointed face, sharp ears, bushy tail, eats ants, sounds kinda cute."

"I thought he meant wombat."

"Nope. Also you do get camels in Australia. And all that stuff about the stone-eating bird? Ed says it's a slightly over-dramatic but reasonably accurate description of a cassowary. And the armed shrimp is a pistol-prawn. They don't really defend themselves against people, but they do snap, crackle, pop and spurt a bit. Oh – and there *are* flying foxes in Sydney. Fruit bats, to you. Quite famous, Ed says."

"I'm speechless."

"So how come you can talk? The point is – whatever weird scenario Mitch is coming up with, maybe you ought to take it seriously. The rest is true – that might be as well."

"This isn't exactly good news," I said. "He's been trying to make me go over there and help him out with something, but he won't say what it is."

"So did you agree?"

"No, because I thought he was just winding me up. But now it looks as if he wasn't . . ."

"Do you have a bad feeling about it?"

"Yes, I do. Especially as he said the power women might think it was illegal – remember?"

"Then don't do it," said Ruth. "Concentrate on Tom."

"He says if I don't help him he'll go it alone and get into difficulties, or danger, or something."

"He's a grown up person," said Ruth. "He isn't your responsibility. I just thought you ought to know about the numbat and all."

"And now I do, it changes things."

"Set Mrs Cooper on him. She'll sort him out."

"I can't. He wants it kept secret. She's so pushy with him, Ruth, you can see he's desperate for a project of his own. It's the only way he'll be able to avoid being walked all over."

"It's his project," said Ruth, "let him sort it out. You've done your bit, you got him there. I only have about twenty seconds left. Listen, I don't want to rush you through your time with Tom, but I'll be glad when you get over here. I think there's something a bit strange happening and I need you to tell me if I'm imagining it or not."

"What kind of strange?"

"Time's run out," said Ruth. "Have fun. See ya."

The line went dead.

When I emerged into the kitchen I found only three of the family there. Tom had gone off to see if the surf was up. It seemed Ruth had got that bit right, anyway.

"You could have had another lie-in," said Tom's mother. "Not that it isn't nice to see you."

"Nothing like an early morning alarming call to get you going," I said.

"You mean early morning *alarm* call," said Melanie.

I said I knew what I meant.

"Wait till I tell them at school I took a call from New York!" said Melanie.

"So do you have any plans for today?" said her father.

I had none at all. But it didn't seem quite right to say so. I didn't want anyone to feel they had to take care of me. Especially Tom. So I said, "I think I'd like to go into central Sydney again."

"Good idea. I'll find you our street map. And I think we have a guidebook somewhere. Can you be back by six? My sister is driving Uncle Mitch over for a full family reunion dinner."

"Oh, no," I said, quite shaken at the thought. "I'll come back at the end of the evening. I won't intrude on a family reunion."

"You'd be more than welcome," said Tom's mother.

"Try and make it," said Tom's father.

"You *be* there," said Melanie, giving me a friendly shove. "You can play with me when it gets boring."

Then all three of them went into crisis-try-and-get-out-of-the-house-on-time mode, so I went for a shower. By the time I was dressed, they'd gone.

I'm not at all worried about Mitch, I told myself, as I ate some breakfast.

I'm not worried about Mitch, I repeated to myself, as I cleared away my mug and plate.

I'm not worried, I muttered, as I collected up the guidebook and checked the instructions for getting into town.

I'm worried, I whispered, as I hitched my bag over my shoulder and then hesitated at the front door.

I dumped my bag, went back into the kitchen, and phoned Mrs Cooper. I planned to ask if Mitch was recovering well from his journey. I just wanted to know that he was safely in her house.

"Where are you?" she said rather tersely when she heard my voice.

I told her.

"Well that's very strange," she said. "Uncle Mitch called a cab for himself and set off not ten minutes ago. He said he was going to meet you. It's fifty years since he was in Sydney and he's over eighty. I most certainly wouldn't have allowed him out on his own if I'd thought you were going to let him down."

Sometimes my brain works really fast. Sometimes it does it when I need it to. I knew that if I told Mrs Cooper the truth, she wouldn't just be furious with me, she'd be furious with him, too. I remembered

him saying that if he came a cropper it would give
her an excuse to put him away. I didn't know if I
believed that or not, but I couldn't risk it.

"Everything's under control, Mrs Cooper," I said.
I straightened my back as I spoke to make sure I
sounded adult and efficient. "Certainly I'm meeting
him. I was just checking that he'd left."

I heard the intake of breath that meant she was
about to say something else, but I gave her no chance.
"*That*'s all right, then," I said. "Thanks so much.
Goodbye." And I hung up.

Sorry, Mitch, I thought, I didn't believe you really
had a plan. I *will* try and help you with whatever it
is you want to do.

Then I sat down on a kitchen stool and clenched
my hands on the counter-top.

How on earth was I going to track down Mitch,
on my own, in a strange city, when I hadn't the
faintest idea where he might have gone?

CHAPTER TWELVE

Mitch Missing

I leant on the kitchen counter and tried to work out a plan.

Perhaps I should go to Mrs Cooper's street and then walk in ever-increasing circles until I found Mitch?

No. It must be fifteen minutes since he left by cab – he could be miles from the house, in any direction. All I'd do would be lose myself as well.

Perhaps I should call the police, say I had an urgent message for him, and let them track him down?

No. Mrs Cooper would go nuts. And Mitch'd never forgive me if I set the law on him.

Perhaps I should phone around the cab firms until I found the one who'd picked him up? Perhaps they'd be able to tell me where they'd taken him?

Yes. That seemed the best option.

There turned out to be an awful lot of cab firms in the Sydney directory. I decided he'd probably have called a local one, so I spread out the City map in the hope of matching up addresses. Then I saw it was a central Sydney map. The suburbs were not covered. So unless I got lucky early, I was going to have to dial every single number. That could take a couple of hours – and what if the controller couldn't remember who'd picked up which fare anyway?

I didn't have a better idea, though, so I reached for the phone.

At that moment, I heard a car pull up outside. There were voices, a door slammed, and the car shot off. Two seconds later the front door opened – and Tom mooched in. His hair was wet. His sweatshirt and jeans had damp patches on them. He was carrying a soggy bundle which dripped on his feet as he walked. He had vivid yellow sunblock cream on his nose. And still he looked good. Life is unfair.

"Hi," he said. "How's your day shaping?"

Badly, I thought, but possibly not as badly as Mitch's.

Aloud I said, "How was the surf?"

"Brilliant," said Tom. "I'd have stayed, but I have a lecture." He walked through to the next room and I heard the splat as the bundle hit the bottom of the bath.

I'd just got over my surprise at seeing him, when he reappeared and headed for the fridge. "Want a juice?" he said. He'd wiped the sunblock off his nose, but he was still very damp.

"No thanks," I said. "I have to make some calls. Mind if I take the phone to my room?"

"Cool," said Tom. Then he hesitated, one hand on the fridge door and the other holding a carton of orange. "You okay?" he said. "You look spaced out."

How could I betray Mitch to Tom? On the other hand, how could I pass up the chance of asking for Tom's help? I stood there, dithering.

I couldn't let him think I was tongue-tied because of his presence. Also, I was getting more worried about Mitch by the second. So I told him the story. I made it brief. I just said Mitch had some plan that he wanted kept secret, that I hadn't taken him seriously, and that now he was on the loose alone. Also that Mrs Cooper wouldn't be launching a search because I'd lied to her.

"I tell you what's really haunting me," I said. "Mitch told me that if he came a cropper it would give his family an excuse to put him away. That would be terrible!"

"Hey – we wouldn't do that!" said Tom.

"It's what he said."

"He's wrong. He's all churned up with the move. He's not thinking clearly. Still, I wouldn't want to see the old guy come a cropper. Can you remember exactly what he told you? Any clues?"

"All I know is it seems to be to do with his inheritance. That part isn't a secret – he was upsetting Mrs C by going on about it that first evening."

"Yeah," said Tom. "They all get edgy when he gets on to that. They're afraid he might contest his old man's will. It isn't the money they care about. The family will pay for whatever he needs. It's just that contesting wills is a messy business. All it does is cause bad feeling. And the only person who gets any loot out of it is the lawyer. Why are you shaking your head?"

"Think back," I said. "He told us at dinner he wasn't going to do that. He said it wasn't *that* inheritance he was talking about."

"Trouble is," said Tom, "that's the only inheritance there ever was."

"I've remembered something else."

"Yeah?"

"He said he was going to look for his roots. It's just struck me – could he have meant his convict roots? Is that why he's being cryptic – because he's embarrassed?"

"Not him!" said Tom. "Anyway, it's respectable now. People get a real kick out of having crims for ancestors."

"What roots could he have meant, then?"

"He was born in Sydney," said Tom, "so he's back with his roots already. All I can think of is the house where he and my grandfather were raised – all those years ago."

"Where is it? I'd better try it."

"Don't know," said Tom. "It was sold years before I was born. I've seen snaps of it, though."

He went through to the sitting room and crouched down by the bookshelves. "They should be here," he said, hauling a couple of dozen photo albums onto the floor and beginning to rake through them.

"A photo of it isn't going to be much good," I said. "I can't jog round the whole of Sydney trying to match a photo to a house! I'd be better off calling all the cab companies."

"It'll be in the oldest album," said Tom, ignoring me. He began flipping through ancient yellowed pages, divided by filmy sheets with patterns of cobwebs on them. "Yes! Here – come and look."

We knelt on the floor side by side and stared at a sepia photograph of an old colonial-style house with gum trees in the garden and a chair on the porch.

"It had character, right enough," said Tom. Gently, he eased the picture loose from its page and turned it over. "Ha!" he said in triumph. On the back, written in pencil, was an address.

"It is a wonderful house," I said. "I can see why Mitch would want to go back."

"I don't know what he thinks he'll do when he gets there, though," said Tom. He got to his feet. Then he held out his hand and hauled me up, too. "There'll have been strangers living in it for donkey's years."

"But he would think of it as his roots, wouldn't he?" I said. "Where is it? Is it far?"

"I don't know the street, I'll have to look it up," said Tom. He strode into the kitchen and lifted a car key down from a hook. Then he headed for the front door. "Come on!" he said, as I stood where I was, not understanding. "Let's move. My street map's in the car."

"But you have lectures," I said weakly.

"My aged relly's gone walkabout," said Tom, "and we're on his case. That's much more important."

We found the street on the map before we drove off. Tom said he could get us to the right suburb so I could look at the scenery for a while. "I'll tell you when you have to start navigating," he said.

I may have forgotten to mention that Tom's house is above a bay and there are sea views in three directions. The first part of the drive was lovely. Then we got on to one of the long boring roads that link the Sydney suburbs, and I lost interest in the landscape.

"I just hope nothing bad's happened to him," I said. "He seems so frail."

"He'll be right," said Tom. "He's a tough old bloke."

"I think he's unhappy," I said. "I know it isn't my business, but I don't know why your family brought him over here. He was fine where he was."

"He wasn't," said Tom. "His letters were getting lonelier and more homesick all the time."

"He had a nice neighbour," I said. "Ruth and I met her."

"Her husband's got a job in Canada. They're set to move. He'd be even lonelier then. He's better here. They're kind, really, the aunts, and my folks'll look after him too."

"I'm sure they will," I said, thinking I meant it.

"You don't sound convinced," said Tom.

I thought some more and realised I wasn't.

"It's just that I don't think your aunt understands him," I said. "She just told me he's confused in his mind, and I sort of believed her at first, but he isn't. He really isn't. We may not know what he's up to at the moment, but I'm sure *he* knows."

"Listen," said Tom, "Mitch is over eighty. My aunt thinks confusion sets in at sixty-five, *always*. When she sees more of him, she'll learn. We're getting close – you want to look at the map?"

I flattened it out on my lap and followed our route with my finger. "Left here, then up to the junction and right," I said. "I hope you're not missing an important class to do this."

"I'll catch up," said Tom. "I had to take time out for the European trip as well, and I caught up okay. I've got mates who lend me notes."

"Straight on here. Then it's next left and that's *it*, that's the street."

"I've just thought," said Tom. "I got to Europe, all expenses paid, because I was on escort duty. And that's how you got here, right?"

"It certainly is."

"So it seems we have something in common after all!"

"It seems we do!" I said.

Tom stopped the car at one end of the crucial road and we turned and grinned at each other. Then we stared down the road.

"Are you sure about this?" said Tom. "It doesn't look right."

I was sure about it, but it certainly didn't look right. Mitch's family house had been large, sprawling and unusual, standing in the middle of a spread of land. This road was lined with modern bungalows with terracotta tiled roofs, each with a garage at one side, each with a neat garden all around.

"It must be right down the other end," I said. "Beyond the bend."

"Okay," said Tom, starting the engine again. "We'll cruise down."

As the car nosed gently round the bend, we both said, "There!" at the same time. We hadn't spotted the big old rambling family mansion, though. What we'd spotted was Mitch, at the far end of the road, leaning on his stick, apparently staring at nothing much.

"He thought this was the right street, too!" said Tom, letting the car drift on towards him.

"It *is* the right street," I said. "I'm a good map-reader. They must have demolished the old houses and built all these."

Tom whistled through his teeth. "You're not wrong," he said. "What a shame."

"I suppose people don't want big houses anymore."

"They do," said Tom. "Especially old ones. But

even in that ancient snap it looked about to disintegrate. Probably a pigeon landed on the chimney and the whole thing fell down."

"Mitch'll be so upset," I said, as Tom stopped the car and we climbed out. "He never expects things to change."

Mitch may have been upset, but also he was furious. With me. "You betrayed me!" he said. "You told the family!' I'll never trust a woman again."

"I only told Tom," I said, shaken.

"You had no right to tell anyone," said Mitch.

"Hey, let up," said Tom, putting one arm round his great-uncle's shoulders and the other round mine. "You *knew* Jo would have to come looking for you. And how could she have found you by herself – a stranger in town without wheels?"

Mitch just grunted.

"I won't tell anyone else," I said. "And neither will Tom. Will you?"

"No way," said Tom. "We'll take you back and we'll let everyone think you and Jo had a nice trip out today, as planned."

"Fair enough," said Mitch. After his brief flash of anger he looked tired and defeated.

"I'm really sorry about the house," I said. "That was what you came to see, wasn't it?"

"I made the cabman drop me two streets away, so I could walk home like I used to," said Mitch wistfully.

"Mitch," said Tom, suddenly looking worried, "you didn't expect to find your family still here, did you?"

Mitch gave him a look of utter scorn. "Course not!" he said.

"How were you going to get home?" I said.

"I hadn't thought that far," said Mitch. "I'll plan better in future."

He wasn't seriously cross with me any more, but I still felt guilty.

He climbed into the front of the car and I got in the back. He stared gloomily at where I assume the old house had stood. Then, as Tom turned the car, he gave one of his secretive chuckles and said, "I wonder if the demo blokes had any surprises!"

It didn't matter what questions we asked him, he wouldn't be drawn into saying anything more.

We drove him home to Mrs Cooper's, and then got trapped there for an hour while she insisted on making us all sandwiches for lunch. Fortunately, she'd run out of prawns.

All that time there was a horrible idea building up at the back of my mind. I didn't want to let it into the front of my mind until I was on my own with Tom. When I *was* on my own with him on the drive back, I still didn't face it. We seemed to be getting on so well – I didn't want to risk spoiling things.

I went into the house while Tom put the car away. Then, when I was alone for a couple of minutes, I faced up to the horrible idea.

It had been set off by the memory of various things Mitch had said – back on the plane as well as back at the vanished house. He'd talked about having a final big row with his father. He'd talked about burying the past and walking away. He'd said I'd be surprised at what he'd buried. Then he'd talked about the people who'd pulled down the old house – and presumably dug up its foundations. He'd said he wondered if *they'd* had any surprises.

What exactly had he buried? Did he really mean the demo men might have had a surprise – or did he mean they might have had a nasty shock!

I went through to the kitchen-end of the room and put the kettle on. As soon as Tom came in I planned to ask him how much he knew of his family's history. I planned to ask if Mitch's father had died of natural causes – or if he'd disappeared.

It seemed an outrageous question, but I just had to hope Tom wouldn't take offence.

How weird, I thought, if Tom and I got it together just as I uncovered a hideous family secret.

Then I saw something that completely distracted me.

On the fridge, held in place with a water-melon-slice-magnet, was a note. It said, "Shelley called back." Then there was a telephone number.

There were only two people in that house who could possibly have rung Shelley and left a message for her to call back. One was me and one was Tom. It hadn't been me.

For one shameful moment I considered 'losing' the note. I'm not that underhand, though.

As Tom walked in at the front door, I didn't offer him tea. I didn't ask if he felt like skiving for the rest of the day and taking me to the beach. I didn't tactfully bring up the subject of his great-uncle's past. I said, in an ultra-casual voice, "Oh, Tom, Shelley wants you to call her. The number's on the note."

Then I went straight to my room.

CHAPTER THIRTEEN

A Slight Misunderstanding

Two seconds after I reached my room, I heard Tom beginning to dial Shelley's number. I realised that with the house as empty and quiet as this I would hear his half of the conversation, and I didn't think I'd like that. So I went and took a shower. Fortunately, the day was so hot that it was unlikely that Tom would think that was an odd thing to do.

I didn't hurry. I even spent some time back in my room choosing which tee-shirt to wear. When I came out, Tom was sitting at the counter. He'd finished making the tea I'd started on. One mug was in his hand, another was beside him on the counter. He pushed it towards me.

"Shelley says one of the staff's having a bit of a barbie in his backyard tonight," he said. "Meet at the office at six. What do you reckon?"

This time my brain did not work fast enough and there was an awkward pause. The trouble was there was too much to think about.

If this was a business invitation from an Australian travel agent to a representative of Quest, then I definitely should go.

If this was a friendly invitation from a local girl to a visitor in town, then it would be nice to go.

On the other hand, if this was an invitation from Shelley to Tom, and they'd only included me because they thought they had to, then I shouldn't go along and crowd them. That would be awful.

"Did Shelley actually ask me?" I said, hoping to get a clearer idea of what I should do.

"Everyone's welcome," said Tom. "We don't do formal invites like you Poms."

He was just sitting there, looking at me, waiting for my answer. I couldn't read his expression. Did he want me there or not?

"Yes, I'll go along," I said. "I really think I should. It could be good for business."

I was rather pleased with that answer. I thought it hit the right note. Whatever Tom and Shelley might feel about each other, neither of them could think I was playing gooseberry. Always assuming they have gooseberries in Australia. And if they decided to spend the entire evening out of sight in the shrubbery, no one else there would have to feel sorry for me. I was not Tom's girl. I was a visiting travel agent.

"Fair enough," said Tom. "I'll drop you off, if you like."

My stomach seemed to fall through a trap door.

"You're going too, aren't you?"

Tom shook his head. "Can't make it," he said.

We did exchange a few more words before he went off to catch an afternoon lecture, but I don't remember what they were. Was I paranoid, or was Tom staying away because I was going? I decided I would never know. Having made a strong case for accepting, I could hardly back off now. I was so flustered that I didn't realise, until far too late, that I had frozen Tom out – right out of the house, in fact.

For the next hour or so, until Melanie got back from school, I sat on the porch, swatting the occasional fly and thinking gloomy thoughts.

Melanie changed all that, and not just because she's good company. She fetched us both a juice and settled down for a gossip. Being under thirteen she didn't beat about the bush, gooseberry or otherwise. She got right to the point.

"Do you like my brother?" she said.

"Of course I do," I said guardedly. "I like all of you."

"No, I mean do you *really* like him?" said Melanie. "He *really* likes you."

I wanted to be straight with her. On the other hand I thought I ought to remember that she'd probably tell him everything I said.

"Did he say that?" I asked.

"I know him," said Melanie confidently. "He likes you a lot. But he won't tell you. Why don't you say you want him to take you on a date?"

I told her about the barbecue.

"Can't he go with you?" said Melanie.

"He said he couldn't make it," I said. "But *I* think he didn't want to go."

Melanie nodded understandingly. "He doesn't like crowds of strangers," she said. It suddenly occurred to me that she was talking as if she were his mother, not his kid sister. "He's really shy," she went on. "Specially around girls. Most especially around girls he likes."

"Mel, he can't *possibly* be," I said, forgetting that

I was going to be careful what I said. "He's so incredibly good-looking, he *cannot* be shy."

"That's *why* he's shy," said Melanie. "See, all the girls think he's vain because of his looks, so they all put him down, to teach him a lesson. But he isn't vain so he just thinks they don't like him. He's never had a regular girl-friend."

"Now listen!" I said. "He wasn't too shy to call Shelley, and he only met her yesterday."

Melanie frowned. "Shelley?" she said. "The one who called you this morning?"

"She didn't call for me," I said. "She was calling your brother."

"It was you she asked for," said Melanie.

I stared at her. "I think I need to run through this from the beginning," I said. "I'm confused."

"When you were in the shower this morning," said Melanie, "this Shelley person called and I put a note on the counter for you."

"On the fridge," I said. "Stuck on with a watermelon-slice-magnet."

"On the *counter*," said Melanie.

"Fridge!"

"Counter!"

She got up and hurried into the house. Half a minute later she was back. "On the floor," she said, handing me a piece of paper with "Ring Shelley" written on it, "*and* on the fridge." She handed me the note I'd seen, the one that said 'Shelley called back'. "This is Mum's writing," she said. "She must have taken this call when she came back at lunchtime."

Shelley had rung back because I hadn't responded to her first message. She'd been calling me all the time. What must she have thought when Tom rang her?

"So why do you think Tom called her?" said Melanie.

"It's too long a story," I said. "I think it's possible I may have misunderstood your brother."

Melanie looked at me faintly accusingly. "He thinks you told him to back off," she said.

"I assumed he was only asking me out because he thought he had to!" I said.

Part of my mind didn't quite believe I was confiding all this to someone so much younger. The other part was glad to talk about it.

"No – he wants to take you out," said Melanie.

"Did he tell you to say this to me?" I said, suddenly suspicious.

"No!" said Melanie, looking hurt. "And he mustn't know what I've said. But if you like him just be nice to him, okay?"

"Okay," I said, suddenly feeling hugely encouraged. "I tell you what, when he gives me a lift to this barbecue tonight, I won't let him drive off, I'll make him stay with me. Will that do?"

"Tonight?" said Melanie. "No. He has to come to Great-Uncle Mitch's special dinner tonight."

I couldn't believe I'd been so stupid. All that agonising about the invitation had been completely unnecessary. I'd been so busy fretting about Shelley and the barbecue that I'd completely forgotten the family reunion.

"You're invited too," said Melanie sternly.

"It was nice of them to ask," I said, "but it'll be better if I'm not there. I'm not family. They'll understand. And I'll just have to try again and ask Tom to spend time with me tomorrow."

"Excellent," said Melanie.

Melanie gave me such a feeling of confidence that I think I really might have turned to Tom, as he drove me into town, and asked him outright for a date. What had I got to lose?

However, Tom didn't drive me in to the party after all. He was so late back from college that his father offered me a ride instead.

Tomorrow, I thought, as Tom's father negotiated the rush hour traffic, I'll talk to Tom tomorrow. Probably. I could feel my confidence beginning to ebb again.

The party was great. Everyone was very friendly and the backyard was so huge it wasn't necessary to stand in the greasy smoke from the grilling steaks like you do in England. In fact, there was only one thing missing.

Shelley noticed he was missing, too. She seemed to think Tom had been calling her for a date, but as she had a steady boy-friend anyway, she hadn't planned to do any more than invite him to the party. So I didn't bother to explain.

She was as nice to me on my own as she had been to both of us in the office. And perhaps I did make useful contacts. I certainly learnt something.

What's the worst that can happen to a Quest tour guide? Getting stuck in a lift trying to take people to the top of a tower for a scenic experience? Failing to find the Roman Remains in a major museum? Spending an hour getting a group to a special restaurant and discovering it's closed for renovations? Misreading a promotional leaflet and finding yourself talking about the Roman Tic Movement or some guy called Egypt Ian?

These people's worst-case scenarios had to do with being scooped out of a boat by a low branch onto the head of a dozing crocodile. Or watching the camping provisions being marched off by a column of ants. Or reaching for the last unused water can on a desert crossing and finding nothing in it but a hole. Or waking up in a hammock with some kind of aggressive and poisonous wildlife dribbling on your chest.

When, finally, three of them walked me up into town and then waved me off in a cab I felt as though I'd been on holiday at last. No Mitch to worry about. No Tom to worry about. Just nice uncomplicated people who let me join in their good time.

This may seem an odd thing to say, but the fact they were all in couples helped, too. I didn't have to fret about whether or not I was going to end up on my own. *I* knew I was. *They* knew I was. So it didn't matter.

When I got back, the family reunion was over. Mitch and Mrs Cooper had gone home. So had Mrs Mackenzie, the slightly less powerful of the power women. Melanie had gone to bed and so had Tom.

Mr and Mrs Mitchell, who were still up, invited me to help finish off the last of the coffee and chocolates.

"How was the barbie?" said Tom's father.

"Great, thanks," I said. "How was the dinner party?"

"All right, I think," said Tom's mother, "but Mitch seemed a bit depressed, we thought. Maybe he's still a little jet-lagged."

I didn't know if he'd told them the house of his childhood had vanished. He certainly hadn't mentioned it to Mrs Cooper when Tom and I delivered him home that morning, so I didn't say anything.

"He was sorry not to see you," said Tom's father. "I think he wrote a note and left it in your room."

When I eventually went to bed, about half an hour later, I found Mitch's note on my pillow.

It said: 'I hope you didn't stay out because I was cranky with you. It was a shock to see the house gone. There's only one thing left for me to do now. Go to mortuary station. Go to see my father. Don't worry – I don't expect you to join me! Mitch.'

I read it three times. I couldn't decide if he meant the only thing left for him to do was wait for death. Or if – surely not – if he meant he was going to hurry his death along a bit.

I screwed it up and pushed it into a drawer. Thank you, Mitch, I thought. Nice one! How do you expect me to sleep now?

CHAPTER FOURTEEN

The End of the Line

I made myself get up extremely early. I had no idea what time Tom left to ride the waves before college, and I desperately wanted to talk to him. He was the only one of the family I felt I could tell about Mitch's note, which had made me very uneasy indeed.

Also, if Melanie was right and he did like me, then I thought I'd better find out fast. My flight on to New York was confirmed. I didn't have much time left in his home town.

I hit it just right. When I walked into the kitchen Melanie was still asleep, her parents were just beginning to turn on taps in the bathroom, and Tom stood alone in the kitchen, contemplating the fridge.

You may wonder why I didn't just bounce up to him and say something like: "Let's be straight with each other. I like you. Do you like me? If so, what are you going to do about it?"

The reason is simple. I was afraid he would say something like, "As far as I'm concerned, you're just someone doing a job for my aunt."

Ridiculous of me, of course. He'd never be so blunt. But he might mumble and avoid answering, and I wouldn't like that.

Yes, I did remember what Melanie had told me, but you can't always believe a little sister. It wasn't that I thought she'd deliberately lie. It was just that by then she'd shown me her room. All her soft toys were arranged with their arms around each other. Her music collection was end-to-end broken-heart ballads. Her favourite books each had a cover picture of a man and a woman gazing at each other. I didn't need a degree in psychology to understand that Melanie was a romantic. Romantics don't necessarily lie, but they don't necessarily recognise the truth, either.

Anyhow, I said nothing romantic to Tom. Just asked him if he could spare a moment to discuss Mitch. He said he could. Then he opened the fridge and poured two orange juices, and I tried not to wish he'd offer to take me to the beach with him while we talked.

"You're always on about Mitch," he said, sitting at the kitchen counter and knocking back his juice. "What's the problem this time?"

"It's sort of about yesterday and Mitch being so depressed. And your parents said he was depressed last night, too."

"He was a bit low-key," said Tom. "But if you remember he *had* just found out they'd bulldozed his past while he wasn't looking. Fair do's – that sort of thing *does* depress a bloke."

"I think it may have been more than that," I said. "Can I ask you something really awful?"

Tom looked startled. "Sure," he said cautiously.

"Do you know how Mitch's father died?" I couldn't quite believe I was really saying this, but I couldn't stop now. "I mean – was there a body and a funeral?"

Tom began to laugh. "Hey, weird lady," he said, "what are you saying? You think he spontaneously combusted or what?"

I didn't laugh. "I wondered if he'd disappeared," I said.

Tom's laughter died away. "Give the bloke a break," he said. "You're not saying you think Mitch did his old man in?"

"No!" I said, feeling horribly flustered, "Well, yes. Well, no. When I think of Mitch I can't imagine that. But he's said such odd things . . . he's talked about bad rows . . . he's talked about burying the past . . ."

"Figure of speech," said Tom.

"And he thought the people who pulled down the house might have found something odd . . ."

"Yes," said Tom, "I did wonder about that . . . but I managed to stop short of suspecting homicide."

"And now he's more gloomy than normal . . ."

"How gloomy is normal?"

". . . and he left me a note all about death."

"His old man's death?"

"No, his own death! And I began to think maybe he did something dreadful all those years ago and he was somehow drawn back to the scene – and now I can't help thinking he's planning suicide."

All the talking and tension had made me overwhelmingly thirsty. I drained my glass at a gulp.

"Now I've said it," I muttered, feeling quite tearful, "I realise how terrible it sounds and I'm really sorry but I had to tell someone and I'm sure I'm wrong in what I'm thinking but I truly am worried about him."

"Don't get upset," said Tom. "You'll cry pure orange juice and make your face sticky."

I started to giggle.

"Oh boy!" said Tom. "Is that humour or hysteria? Listen, tell me what Mitch said about killing himself."

"He didn't actually say that – just said that there was nothing left for him but death."

"Those were his exact words?"

"No – he sort of wrapped it up. Said all that was left was to go and see his father. Well his father's not in the land of the living, is he? And then something about going to death row, or cemetery junction or something. I can't remember – I'll get the note."

When I came back with the crumpled paper, Tom took it from me and smoothed it out. "Mortuary Station!" he said.

"Yes, mortuary station. That's a euphemism for death, isn't it?"

"No," said Tom. "It isn't. It's a Victorian building down at Central. Trains used to run from there up to Rookwood Cemetery."

"Used to?"

"The line hasn't been used for about fifty years, but it was probably on the go when Mitch was last here. His father's buried out there. This note's saying he's going to visit his father's grave, that's all!"

Before I could feel as stupid as I deserved to, he went on, "But he shouldn't go on his own. We haven't taken him on a city-up-date tour yet."

"He is a bit out of date, isn't he?"

"Too right. The harbour skyline is about thirty years old – he may have seen pics but he's never seen the real thing – it could freak him out."

"This is getting worse."

"I'll call him up," said Tom, "and tell him we'll drive him out there."

I noticed the 'we', but I didn't comment.

"Not yet, though," Tom went on. "It's too early."

He abandoned his surfing plans, and the two of us rounded up a cooked breakfast for five. This went down very well with the rest of the family. In fact I still remember it as one of the best times we all had together – until Tom's father spoilt it by saying, "Will you look at those two, clearing the table together, just like an old married couple."

If we'd been more at ease with each other we could have laughed it off. But at that point we weren't, and we couldn't. And when Tom's mother said, "Don't embarrass them," she only made things worse.

In the middle of our shared moment of social unease, the telephone rang. Mrs Cooper was on the other end. She was frantic. Mitch had disappeared.

Not surprisingly, he had left behind one of his disturbing notes. This one said, "Don't worry. If it works out I'll tell you all about it. If it doesn't you'll probably read about me in the local rag."

Pandemonium set in.

"Ease up," said Tom. "We know where he's gone. We'll go get him."

And that is how I ended up walking hand in hand with Tom through Rookwood Necropolis, Sydney's ginormous city of the dead.

We didn't go straight there, of course. First we drove along the fumy, traffic-clogged road to Central to check out Mortuary Station.

If I hadn't known better, I'd have thought it was a little Victorian church, abandoned among the grimy modern downtown buildings. But even Mitch, who had obviously thought it was still functioning, would have been able to see at once that no trains called here any more.

"No sign of him," said Tom. "He must have got a bus – or maybe a cab."

Then we drove out to Rookwood.

I knew what I was expecting. I've been in a cemetery before. I was expecting lots of graves, and maybe some stone angels, with possibly a little chapel somewhere in the middle. I was also sure we would catch sight of Mitch right away, standing by his father's headstone.

No chance.

We were faced with a vast estate, spread all over a high plateau, with streets and road signs, car parks and bus shelters. Not so much a graveyard, more an underground suburb with unusually quiet residents.

Tom stopped the car in the first car park and we got out. The sun thundered down on us. A bus rolled slowly past sending up a small cloud of dust. Rookwood stretched to the horizon and vanished beyond it.

"How will we find him?" I said, staring blankly around.

"I have no idea," said Tom. "I've never been here before."

"Well, where do we start?"

"I'm sorry, this is my fault," said Tom. "I went for the dramatic exit. I should have asked for directions before I drove off! You want to cruise around or you want to walk?"

"I think we should walk. We could miss him from the car."

That was when he reached out and took my hand.

"This may not be the kind of sightseeing you had in mind," he said, "but you have to admit it's different!"

We passed through the old section quite early on, without seeing any sign of Mitch. Then somehow we went on into areas where he couldn't possibly be. We found the Russian Orthodox memorials, with the miniature gold onion domes on top. We found the Maori lawn, the Chinese quarter and whole streetfuls of Italian tombs, like small marble houses.

"Let's go back to the first bit," I said eventually. I'd been thinking about the old graves, with their tombstones and crosses not quite straight. They reminded me of an English country churchyard, but on a rather grand scale. "Isn't that where they'll have buried his father?"

"That's what I thought," said Tom. "But we already looked there."

"It would have been easy to miss him, though," I said. "This place is so huge it swallows people up."

"Yuck!" said Tom. "What a gruesome thought."

We were quite close to Mitch before we spotted him. He was almost hidden by the Mitchell family tombstone – not because it was particularly large but because he was kneeling down beside it. He didn't notice us.

Tom, who is a lot taller than I am and could see over the stone, gave a sort of strangled grunt. Then he clenched his hand on mine so tightly that I squeaked. "He's gone troppo!" he said. "Look what he's doing!"

"What?" I said, as we closed in.

"He's digging!" Tom hissed at me.

He was, too. He was holding a trowel in both hands and hacking at the dry ground with its point.

I felt as though I was in a nightmare. All I could think was that Mitch planned to unearth his dead father and demand his lost inheritance.

"We have to stop him," I said, pulling free of Tom's hand and running towards the grave.

"And fast!" said Tom, running behind me. "There's a cop car cruising this way and I think they've seen him!"

CHAPTER FIFTEEN

Mitch's Secret

Mitch looked up as we reached him. He didn't seem particularly surprised to see us – just faintly irritated.

On the road behind him, I saw the police car slow down.

"I had to buy a new one of these," he said, waving his trowel at us. Then he scooped more earth out of the small pit he'd already made and dumped it on a pile at his side.

The car stopped. Both policemen were looking our way.

"I had a perfectly good one," said Mitch, "and a small fork as well, but you made me leave them behind."

I moved rapidly round to the other side of the grave to block their view.

"I'd dumped them by the fence," said Mitch, "where the old house should have been. I didn't realise I'd left them behind until you'd driven me all the way back."

"Mitch!" said Tom, "you have to stop digging. The cops are here!"

The doors of the police car opened and both officers got out.

Mitch snorted. "Some busybody was staring at me earlier," he said. "I saw her talking on her mobile as she left – she must have called them."

The two policemen began to walk towards us. They were not hurrying. I realised that, from their angle, all they could see were three people near a grave. It was possible they didn't suspect us of anything yet. It was possible they were just coming over to ask if we'd seen anything suspicious.

"Distract them a second," I hissed at Tom.

If he'd hesitated, all would have been lost. He didn't, though. He was terrific. He strode to meet them, saying, "Great day, isn't it?"

"It is," said the first policeman. "Too good to be working, right?"

While Tom kept them talking, and facing away from me, I sidled backwards to the grave behind me. I'd noticed that someone had left a large sheaf of flowers on it.

Tom held their attention for ten seconds. I only needed five.

By the time they reached us, all they could see was an old man kneeling respectfully by a family memorial, with me (granddaughter, perhaps) standing protectively at his side. The fresh flowers on the ground beside the kerbstone just added to the general impression of a family behaving normally in a cemetery. Unless, by some horrible chance, someone moved the sheaf, there was no way they could guess it was hiding Mitch's excavations, not to mention his small shovel.

"G'day," said the second policeman. "We've had a report of vandalism out here – someone desecrating a grave."

"Surely not," said Mitch, rising from his reverent position, with some help from me, and more from the first policeman who rushed forward to offer his arm. "Well I've been here for some time and I'm sure I'd have noticed if anything was amiss."

"My great-uncle has just come back to live in Sydney after fifty years overseas," said Tom chattily. "He's here to visit his father." He indicated the headstone.

"Good on yer, mate," said the second policeman. The first policeman echoed him.

Then they looked around, decided the call had been a hoax, wished us well, and loped back to their car, quite satisfied.

We stood gazing down at the grave until they had driven off and right out of sight. Then I grabbed the flowers and hurried them back where I'd found them. "Excuse me," I whispered to the unknown dust under the ground, "no offence meant, but it was an emergency."

When I turned back, Mitch was down on his knees again, digging like a terrier, and Tom was holding him by the shoulder, obviously trying to pull him back without hurting him.

I hurried over and caught at his digging hand. "You can't *do* this," I said.

Mitch shook my hand off.

"Cool it," he said, "I'm not digging up bones. Can't you see I'm working outside the kerbstone!"

That was true, but he was very close to it.

"I'm only after what's mine," he said, as Tom and I gave up and shrugged at each other over his crouching figure. "After the numbat-watching and the camel-racing, I did a bit of mining in the Northern Territories."

The pile of earth was growing alarmingly.

"I didn't tell you that, young Jo, did I? And I was quite successful. Could have flogged them on site, of course, dealers used to come round every month, but I thought I might get stung. Brought them back to the city instead, to get the best price. Hah!"

We both jumped.

Then Mitch reached into the hole he had made, and pulled out a drawstring bag, full of something lumpy.

"These are good!" said Mitch. He fiddled with the strings until Tom lost patience and untied them for him. "Now help me up again."

When he was standing, he made Tom hold out his hands, and then emptied half a dozen small rocks into them. They were rough and dark, but where the sun caught them they gleamed dully green with tiny flashes of red.

"Wait till you see 'em polished," said Mitch.

"What are they?" I said. "Diamonds?"

"Opals," said Tom, staring at them. "Huge opals."

"Not as precious as diamonds, it's true," said Mitch, "but top quality opals still fetch real money."

"They certainly do,' said Tom. He passed one to me. "Just looks like a bit of rock," he said, "unless you know what it really is."

"I don't think it does," I said. "I wouldn't have known what it was, but I think I'd have known it was something special. Mitch, can I ask you an obvious question?"

"You may," said Mitch, retrieving his opals and dropping them back into the drawstring bag.

"Why did you bury them?"

"When I got back from my 'Missing Years', all my debts had caught up with me. The creditors were closing in. They were threatening to seize my assets. My only assets were my opals and I didn't fancy having them seized, so I hid 'em. Half under the old house, half at the side of the grave, here. I'd planned to get you to help me dig 'em up, young lady, but you wanted to know too much and I didn't want to say anything till I was sure they were still here."

"It's amazing they were," I said. "Why didn't they find them when they buried your father?"

"My father was already dead from a heart attack by the time I got back from the bush," said Mitch. "I came out to the grave to say goodbye to him – and that gave me the idea of where to hide the rest of the stones."

"I thought you told me you had a really big fight with your father and that's when you left Oz!"

"No, love," said Mitch, "you weren't paying attention. I said I left because of the biggest fight of all. I meant the Second World War! I joined up. My old man was already dead by then, rest his soul."

"Mrs Cooper said there was a feud between you and your father that never got patched up."

"Family stories get confused," said Mitch. "My father and I had fights, but it never meant all that much. We were just two males who couldn't share our territory. All quite natural."

"He cut you out of his will, though," said Tom.

"Oh, sure, fair enough. He did that because he said I was no good with money. Told my brother to see I didn't starve. That's why my nieces think they have to look after me, pay my fees in some old crocks home. But I prefer to be independent." He rattled the bag of opal-ore. "And now I can be." He patted the headstone affectionately. "It gave me great pleasure to get Dad to look after my stones for me. It was good to prove I could get my hands on loot and not squander it all."

"Shame he never knew that," said Tom.

"Oh, he knows, wherever he is, he knows. Now would you two young people like to tidy up the mess I've made, please."

Tom and I knelt down and began to scoop the earth back into the hole.

"Why didn't you come back and get these years ago?" I said. "Was it because of the debts?"

"No. The war wiped out the debts. I met my wife in England and kind of started life all over. I had a good job, I travelled, I kept meaning to call back home, but I never quite got round to it. And the longer I left it the harder it became."

Tom and I stood up and began to stamp the earth flat.

"In a way," said Mitch, "there wasn't much to come back for. My parents were dead, my brother was killed in the war, my nieces and nephew were being brought up by their mother and her parents. But I knew I'd get here in the end and I knew my inheritance was waiting for me."

We all stood back and looked at the family grave. Tom and I had done a neat job. No one would have known it had been disturbed."

"It wasn't *all* waiting for you," said Tom.

"No," said Mitch, "I hadn't allowed for half of it ending up as a bonus for a gang of construction workers, but never mind, no worries, I have enough."